THE BARKS & BEANS CAFE
MYSTERY SERIES

SPILLED MILK

THE BARKS AND BEANS CAFE MYSTERY SERIES:
BOOK 4

HEATHER DAY GILBERT

Series: Gilbert, Heather Day. Barks & Beans Cafe Mystery; 4

Subject: Detective and Mystery Stories; Coffeehouses—Fiction; Dogs—Fiction Genre: Mystery Fiction

Author Information & Newsletter: http://www.heatherdaygilbert.com

FROM THE BACK COVER

Welcome to the Barks & Beans Cafe, a quaint place where folks pet shelter dogs while enjoying a cup of java...and where murder sometimes pays a visit.

The fall flea market has arrived in Macy's small mountain town, and she's taking a day off work to check out the local wares. As she and her Great Dane, Coal, wander through the booths, Macy's more than a little taken aback to discover that her enigmatic tattooed barista, Kylie, is selling antique weapons at the event.

She's even more shocked when Coal sniffs out a dead body...and the man appears to have been struck down by one of Kylie's swords.

As rumors begin to circulate, the Barks & Beans Cafe also takes a hit. Customers are reluctant to order their mochas from a murderess. Macy stands by her employee, but even she believes there's a whole lot more to Kylie's history than the woman lets on. To make matters worse, Macy's brother Bo is out of the country, leaving the cafe's future in her hands.

And then her ex-husband Jake shows up, begging to make amends.

With the past rearing its ugly head, Macy has to ignore Jake's distractions, appease the angst of her nervous customers, and convince Kylie to trust her, all before an elusive killer strikes again.

Join siblings Macy and Bo Hatfield as they sniff out crimes in their hometown...with plenty of dogs along for the ride! The Barks & Beans Cafe cozy mystery series features a small town, an amateur sleuth, and no swearing or graphic scenes. Find all the books at heatherdaygilbert.com!

The Barks & Beans Cafe series in order:
Book 1: No Filter
Book 2: Iced Over
Book 3: Fair Trade
Book 4: Spilled Milk
Book 5: Trouble Brewing

Dedicated to my great aunt Jenny Lee, who went home to Glory this year. I can't count all the deep talks we shared about mountain life, family, and writing. You were able to capture what counted with your stories and poems, and I'll go on reading them until I see you again. You were a titan in my life and in so many others.

1

"Hey, mate, how 'bout you throw another steak on the barbie for me," Summer joked.

Chuckling at Summer's affected Australian accent, my brother Boaz—"Bo" for short—obligingly placed another marinated steak on the grill.

Not only was Summer the local animal shelter owner, but as of the end of last month, she was officially Bo's girlfriend. And since Summer was also a good friend to me, their relationship was something I could totally get behind—unlike Bo's short-lived engagement to his thankless ex-fiancée, Tara. It had taken him over a year and a half to put Tara behind him, and I was glad he finally had.

This evening, Bo was hoping we could brainstorm our upcoming one-year anniversary celebration of the Barks & Beans Cafe. It was hard to believe how much our business had blossomed after opening in September of last year.

I thought back over the sacrifices Bo had made to get here. Halfway through last year, he had shocked me by taking early retirement as vice president at his California coffee import business and moved back to our hometown, where he set about renovating our great aunt Athaleen's house. Surprising me even further, he had turned the front half of the oversized Colonial into a cafe that showcased shelter dogs, expressly so I could live my dream of working with canines for the rest of my life.

And that dream had held true, even as we threw ourselves into the logistics of running the cafe. Every day I got to spend with the dogs was a good day for me, no matter how out of control they got. Watching them find their forever homes made me feel we were touching our small West Virginia hometown for the better.

As Summer arranged her baked potatoes on the picnic table next to the salad I'd brought, I leaned back in Bo's pale turquoise rocking chair. Mirroring the interior of his bungalow-style house, his deck furniture was painted in sun-kissed, beachy tones.

"Now this is my idea of service." My Great Dane, Coal, sat in front of me, so I stretched my legs out over his long black spine before tucking them under me. "Thanks for doing the steaks, bro—although I know you wouldn't want me wrecking them, anyway."

Bo laughed, his sky blue eyes crinkling. "You mean like that time you tried to serve me those leather slabs you called steaks?"

"In my defense, the online shop said they were the best cuts of filet mignon," I said.

Bo coughed. "Processed garbage," he said behind his hand.

I didn't pay him much mind. Bo ordered all his beef from a local farmer, and he always made sure he shared it with me. I'd just run out of steak that time and made the bad decision to improvise with something new.

Summer added ice to a glass of sweet tea and propped a decorative peppermint leaf against the rim. She handed it to Bo, and as he accepted it, Summer complimented his grilling savvy. A slight blush crept up beneath his trim red beard, coloring his freckled cheeks. While I knew Summer and Bo were basically crazy about each other, I appreciated that they never got too sappy-sweet around me. Both of them understood I was still recovering from my unexpected divorce with my cheating husband at the start of last year. I didn't really care to recall those days when Jake and I were draped all over each other.

Summer turned to me. "Macy, I've been thinking about doing some kind of adopt-an-animal day at the cafe for the anniversary blowout, but if we add shelter cats to the daily doggie mix, it might turn into chaos."

I looked down at Coal, who turned his wistful amber eyes up at me. "Look at my oversized docile baby. You know he gets along just fine with Bo's crazy kitty."

Bo piped up and tried to defend his wild Calico's honor. "Yeah, but you know Coal is just a chicken when it comes to Stormy. She basically dominated your big lug when she was just a kitten. The shelter dogs and cats aren't used to being out of their kennels for long, much less interacting with each other. And just think of what happened with Waffles."

We all took a moment of silence to remember what had happened when the incorrigible Labradoodle had jumped the divider wall in the cafe. She'd been so spastic that even my longsuffering brother had demanded she go back to the shelter immediately, and that was saying something.

It wasn't the first time Waffles had been returned to the

shelter due to her inability to assimilate into indoor life. After that adventure, she'd been taken in at a farm where she could be outside, so Summer and I had hoped she would settle in well. But even there, she'd pushed her boundaries and ignored commands until the foster parents had brought her back to the shelter.

"Is she with someone now?" I asked, truly hoping she was. She was a sweet dog, albeit as unpredictable as an early October snowstorm.

Summer gave a slow nod. "She is for now. A family with kids came into the shelter and adopted her last week. You can imagine that since she's a purebred, not to mention that gorgeous golden color, she's always the first to get noticed. And you know she loves children. It doesn't look like a lot of drawbacks on the surface."

Bo nodded. "But when people get her home..."

"It's usually another story," Summer finished. "I told them up front about her bathroom accidents and about her tendency to run all over the place, so they can't say they weren't warned. We'll see how long it lasts."

"At least she'll enjoy her time with the kids," I mused. Once again, I wished I could adopt the roving maniac dog, but I knew she'd never be a good fit with my loyal Dane, who liked getting all my attention.

Bo served up the steaks. Summer and I joined him at the picnic table and started filling our plates. Ever the considerate boy, Coal moved toward the edge of the deck and casually stretched out. Although the smell of the steaks was mouthwatering, he hid his interest well, licking his lips only every now and then.

After praying, Bo suggested, "We could always have Milo post the cats' pictures online or share the shelter website page for people looking for felines. Then we could bring in a few extra shelter dogs that Saturday for customers to interact with." Milo was our techie-inclined barista, and he was always plugged into new ways to reach customers.

"That would work well," Summer said. "Are you planning any special foods or coffee drinks for the occasion? Or maybe gift baskets?"

I chewed my butter-soft bite of steak before answering. "Well, remember those baskets we made up for the Girl's Day Out event? They cost way more than I'd anticipated. I don't think we'll go the basket route this time. Instead, I'm thinking we could do a buy-one-get-one-free drink offer, then we'll figure out a special anniversary drink that'll feature our best Costa Rican beans."

"Kylie and I can work on that," Bo said around a ketchup-laden bite of potato.

"What about special decorations?" Summer asked, a neatly-packed bite of salad poised on her fork.

"I've asked Bristol to handle that. She's so good about those kinds of things, and I'm definitely not. Decorating our Christmas trees with old ornaments and putting wreaths up is about as coordinated as I get." Our sweet employee Bristol was not only a gifted dog whisperer in the Barks section of the cafe, but she also had a flair for design that showed up in everything she did.

Summer gave a little clap of her hands. "Perfect! I'm looking forward to getting even more animals into good homes."

Bo's phone rang. He reluctantly looked at the caller ID, then wiped his mouth with a napkin and picked up. "Hatfield here," he said, which indicated he was likely talking to someone from the DEA.

Just last year, Bo had finally admitted that not only had he been the vice president at Coffee Mass, but during that time, he'd also been an undercover agent with the Drug Enforcement Administration. I shouldn't have been surprised, given his Marine background, but it definitely blindsided me. Thankfully, he had also retired early from the DEA. However, there were still some loose ends in regard to criminals he'd come into contact with over the years, and sometimes the DEA called him to ask for or to share information.

One particularly evasive criminal, Leo Moreau, had never been caught. Moreau kept showing up in our lives, which wasn't hard to do since he ran a criminal network in southern West Virginia. Whether he'd built his network *before* he tracked Bo to our hometown or after, I wasn't sure. All I knew is that the man hated Bo because he'd gotten too close to him more than once. Moreau viewed him as the biggest threat to his criminal empire.

Summer and I were whispering with each other when Bo hung up. He took a long drink of iced tea, then stared off into space. I fell silent and Summer followed suit, giving him a chance to explain what was going on.

As if sensing Bo's uncharacteristic distraction, Coal stood and walked over to my brother. Leaning against Bo's thigh, he nudged his nose under Bo's forearm where it rested on the table.

Bo gave him a distracted head pat. That's when I felt certain that whatever it was, it was serious. My brother never did anything halfway or distracted. He'd also never liked Coal putting his wet nose on him for affection.

His eyes sought mine. "Yeah. That was the DEA. My old boss—we just call him Thunder—said that thanks to the tip

Anne Louise gave me last month, they've finally located an official in Ecuador by the last name of Carson."

Last month, following a fiasco at the West Virginia state fair, Leo Moreau's wife, Anne Louise, had given me an unexpected call—unexpected because no one was supposed to be able to find my number. In her sugary sweet southern accent, she'd informed me that my brother needed to look into a guy named Carson in Ecuador.

Our FBI friend, Titan McCoy, felt sure Anne Louise was gearing up to go against her mobster husband, and this was the first step in pinning him to the wall. So the DEA had been actively searching for a lead. Apparently, they'd found it.

Summer, who was up to speed on the Moreau story, said, "That's good news, isn't it? Now they can send someone down to look into him?"

Bo nodded, his lips tight. "That someone is going to be me."

Summer's brown eyes widened.

I gave a frantic shake of my head. "No way. You're not going to do that, Bo. You're out! You're retired. They can't ask this of you."

He gave me a longsuffering big brother look. "Well, obviously anyone can keep an eye on him, but if he's pulled in for interrogation, I'm in the best position to do it, since I basically have a connection with Anne Louise. It's a unique angle that might make him more likely to talk."

I crossed my arms. "It's *really* nice of Anne Louise to put you in this situation. She's probably just using you like a pawn in some twisted takeover game with her husband."

He nodded. "Yes, Titan and I do suspect that she's planning a mutiny of sorts, but we also feel that this is our best opportunity to put a kingpin behind bars for good. Not only is Leo running drugs, stolen valuables, and maybe even trafficking women through the state, but he's also a ruthless murderer—whether he's doing the deed or delegating that job to someone under him. Trust me, we'll thwart Anne Louise before she rises up to fill her husband's shoes."

I recalled how she sounded on the phone—snake-smooth and fearless. "You sure about that?"

Bo frowned. "Sis, I know the timing isn't ideal. It's honestly the last thing I want to do right now. But I have no choice. It's the *right* thing to do." With no preamble, he shoved his chair back and headed inside.

"He's overwhelmed," Summer murmured.

She didn't have to explain Bo to me, although I figured she was just talking things through out loud. My brother hated one thing above all else, and that was losing control. He had no control in this situation, but he knew his duty, and that would have to be enough.

2

THE NEXT MORNING, a full ten minutes before our meet time, I heard my brother unlock the back door and let himself inside. Knowing Bo was always welcome in this house, Coal didn't even bark—although he did let out a small whimper that was presumably directed at Bo's cat. I was going to get the privilege of watching the headstrong Calico while he was traveling.

"Help yourself to coffee," I shouted from the bathroom, where I was making every attempt to whip my fluffy strawberry blonde waves into shape. I was grateful that Bristol had agreed to fill in for me in the Barks section this morning so I could drive Bo to the airport.

"Already had some," he said.

As I hurried to rub oil into my hair, hoping it would push it down a little, I kicked myself for not getting up earlier. After all, I knew full well that Bo never liked to get places late—or even on time. It was his habit to arrive at least fifteen minutes early, so he could map out the situation before anyone else did. He claimed it gave him the upper hand. I'd seen proof positive that he was right about that, but it didn't stop me from consistently running behind. I blamed youngest child syndrome.

I shrugged my long cardigan on over top of my white shirt and jeans, hoping my outfit came off more fashionista than slapdash. Hurrying downstairs, I said, "Sorry it took me so long."

Bo was busy setting up Stormy's favorite carpeted cat tower by my living room window. He pulled Stormy from her crate and gently eased her onto her perch. Her bright green eyes flicked around the room and came to rest on me. She gave a plaintive *meow.*

Coal eased his huge body down near Stormy, his eyes bright and his ears in their permanently pricked-up position. They'd been cropped as a puppy for show purposes, but his owner had met with an unfortunate fate, thus landing Coal in the shelter where I'd latched onto him. I felt incredibly blessed to have stumbled onto just the right rescue dog when I was at one of my lowest points.

"They'll be fine," I assured Bo. "Now that she's getting toward a year old, she's been more calm."

Bo gave a snort. "It's not Stormy I worry about. Coal could accidentally squash her, and he wouldn't even know it."

I shook my head, knowing my Dane would do nothing of the sort. "He considers her his pack now. He won't let any harm come to her."

Bo sighed as if he'd worn himself out going through potential disaster scenarios. "Yeah, you're probably right. Okay, so I set her litterbox in your laundry room, along with a fresh box of litter if you need it. I'm honestly not sure how long I'll be gone. And I put that safety gate in front of it so Coal can't get into it."

My nose wrinkled as I anticipated my new poop-scooping duties, but Bo rushed on. "Don't worry, sis, I cleaned it for ya first." He winked.

As Coal stood and gave Stormy a hesitant sniff, she gave a protracted yowl and arched her back at him. "Sit down, boy," I said. "Give her time."

Obedient as always, Coal did exactly as he was told and proceeded to feign indifference toward the feisty feline.

"See, they'll be fine," I assured Bo. "Don't worry about them. Besides, you can just call me anytime for updates."

He shook his head. "Sorry, Macy, but I can't call you regularly. I'll have to use a burner phone, too. I'll try to squeeze in a call or two, but when we talk, you can't mention anything about what I'm doing down there. Basically, the less contact I have with the outside world, the better."

Noting the grim set of his jaw, I felt a creeping realization that this mission could last awhile. "You're going deep undercover," I said quietly.

His lips twisted into a half-smile. "I don't think you know what that means, but yes, I'll be undercover. You can contact Titan if you need to reach me for any emergency reason—you have his number, right?"

"Yes, I do." In fact, I had to restrain myself from texting Titan on those late nights when I sat awake, pondering the injustices of life. He was easy to talk to, and he seemed interested in me...although he hadn't formally asked me out yet. Like me, he'd been divorced, but he had a tendency to clam up when I mentioned it.

Still, despite his mysterious persona, I knew Titan would be right there if I called, and that was the kind of backup I was going to need while Bo was so far away, doing incredibly dangerous work.

Bo leaned down, giving Stormy a kiss on the black patch on her forehead that extended to the tip of her nose. "Be good," he whispered. As he turned and looked at me, fresh resolve filled his eyes. "Okay, let's get going. My luggage is sitting on the porch, so I'll need to load it into your car."

"Gotcha," I said, snatching my keys and purse from the kitchen counter. For Bo to truly focus on the cafe, he was going to have to get Leo Moreau out of his life forever, and this trip seemed the best way to go about it. I wasn't about to stand in his way.

By the time I closed the cafe Tuesday evening, I was ready to head home and cocoon myself in a blanket with a lighthearted romance book and a warm mug of cocoa. It had been a long afternoon. Not only did our best barista, Kylie, mix up two customer orders in the cafe, but the hound dog in the Barks section acted like he was compelled to howl any time there was an extended period of silence.

His mournful bays echoed in my head as I unlocked the door that connected my half of the house with the cafe. I rarely used the connector, instead favoring a brisk daily walk down the sidewalk that gave onto my enclosed back garden. But today I was exhausted and ready to relax.

Coal met me the moment I stepped inside. His gold-brown eyes were uneasy, as was his body language. He was panting as if he'd been running around the house, and he didn't want to sit down so I could pet him.

In other words, he was telling me something was wrong.

Realization only took a moment to sink in. Stormy. Something must've happened to Stormy.

I started calling for the high-strung cat. "Here, kitty, kitty," I shouted, barreling down the hallway into the living room. There was no sign of the Calico on her perch.

Next, I checked the laundry room, but she wasn't with her litter box or food. I methodically went through every room with my wheedling calls. "Please come out, Stormy. Where are you?"

Coal dragged his feet behind me, as if worn out from his own cat hunt attempts. Hoping I could tap into his doggie sense of smell, I turned back to him. "Where is she, boy? Where'd the kitty go?"

He focused on me a moment, then padded off toward the laundry room. He stood in the middle of it, whining.

It was a small room, and Stormy was nowhere to be seen. Unless...

Taking a small running leap, I jumped on top of the washing machine. As I peered down into the dark, tiny space behind the laundry machines and the wall, sure enough, I caught sight of a multicolored fluffball. Stormy had huddled into the impossibly small space between the dryer exhaust pipe and the wall. She looked up at me and glared, as if I were intruding upon her alone time.

Irritation filled me. "Thanks a lot for letting me know where you were, punk," I said. It wouldn't be a far stretch for the long cat to knock my dryer pipe from the wall, which would be difficult for me to pull out and fix.

I was pondering ways to get to Stormy when there was a knock on the door. It must be someone I knew, since most of my closer friends knew that Coal went a little nuts if they rang the doorbell. Coal gave a quick bark and loped out, and I followed him.

I opened the door to see my new neighbor, Vera Cox, standing outside. She and Auntie A had been close friends back in the day, and she'd recently moved back to town. She tucked a strand of short gray hair behind her ear and held out a dish covered in tin foil.

"I made some extra blackberry cobbler, and I felt like I needed to share it with you for some reason." Her large brown eyes had a twinkle in them.

I grinned and placed my hand under the potholder. "This was just the right day for it, actually. Thank you so much."

She looked concerned. "Anything wrong, dear?"

I set the cobbler on the counter. "Work was a little stressful, and Bo had to fly out of town this morning. Please, come on in."

Nodding, Vera stepped into my kitchen, which connected with my living room. Coal sat down next to her, hoping for an ear scratch from one of his favorite new friends.

Vera obliged him. "He's such a sweet big boy," she crooned. "I'm glad you have him to keep you company. I'm sorry it's been such a rough day, Macy." She glanced around and gave a small clap. "Why, what a beautiful kitty!"

I followed her gaze to the window. Sure enough, Stormy was sitting on her perch, casually licking her paws as if she'd never done anything amiss.

"Oh, she is," I said between gritted teeth. "Beautiful and dangerous."

Vera didn't hear my mutterings because she'd already

walked over to stroke Stormy's head. The Calico sat stock-still, as if reveling in the adoration.

"It gets lonely all by myself in the big house," Vera lamented. "I want to have you over sometime for Parcheesi."

I couldn't claim to know anything about the board game, but I did know a longer-lasting remedy for Vera's solitude.

"You should come by the cafe sometime," I suggested. "Maybe you'll find a shelter dog you'll connect with."

She nodded. "You know, I'll think on that. A dog would liven things up over there. What with my kids living so far away and no grandkids in the foreseeable future, I'm liable to be alone a long time."

I could sense her despondency. "You know you're always welcome here," I said, making a mental note to invite her over for a meal once Bo got home. He was far better cook than I was.

She walked over to stand by me. Although I was only five foot three, Vera was a couple inches shorter and built like a strong wind could carry her on into the next county. She placed an age-spotted hand on my own and said, "You're a sweetie. Your aunt Athaleen would be proud, honey." She stood straighter. "Alright. You enjoy that cobbler and I hope your brother gets back soon." After giving Coal a final pat and stepping onto the porch, she turned and gave me a final grin. "By the way, how are things going with that tall man?"

Vera had seen Titan McCoy after the fair last month, and apparently he had made a lasting impression. It wasn't hard to do for a handsome man who was six foot five. But after watching us interact, Vera was convinced that Titan and I had some kind of special connection.

I could only hope that was true.

"I haven't seen him lately, but we do stay in touch." I

didn't elaborate that we were *so* loosely in touch that the local art gallery owner, Dylan Butler, had been dating me in the meantime. While I really liked Dylan and always enjoyed my time with him, I couldn't overcome the feeling that I needed something...more.

As Vera made her way down my back porch steps, I said, "Thank you again."

She shot me an astute look as she headed down my garden path. "Sometimes it's darkest before the dawn, you know."

I was sure she was talking about Titan, but a chilly wave washed over me, bringing with it an unwanted sense of foreboding. A handful of times in my life, I'd subconsciously pieced actions and conversations together in such a way that I knew ahead of time that something bad was coming down the pike. The times when I'd chosen to ignore that feeling, I'd lived to regret it.

I shivered, drawing back inside and locking the door. I took a moment to pray for Bo, hoping my premonition didn't have any relation to his safety.

Trying to shake off my dread, I headed toward the laundry room, determined to focus on kitty-proofing the area behind my machines. Coal walked alongside me, an understanding look in his eyes. While my Great Dane was a fantastic companion, sadly he couldn't protect me from most things in life.

I only hoped that whatever was coming—*if* something was indeed coming—would good and well wait until my big brother got home.

3

THE REST of the week seemed to drag by, although it did hold some highlights. Kylie didn't botch another order, our baker Charity heard that she was on the judge's October schedule to officially adopt her five-year-old grandson, and Titan sent a text letting me know Bo was safely settled in Ecuador.

However, Stormy had devoted all her waking hours toward squeezing into every inaccessible space she could think of. Part of me understood why she resented Coal's constant need to stand sentinel—after all, Great Danes were working class dogs, bred to guard and rescue and generally make themselves useful to humans, so Stormy had unintentionally provided Coal with a full-time job.

But her antics were getting more and more risky. Although I'd spread flattened boxes over the backs of the laundry machines to keep her out, she'd since discovered she could squeeze behind the fridge. I had to call my bulky barista Jimmy over to help me scoot the appliance back so I could poke her out with the broom handle.

Then, the very next day, she nudged her way into the cabinet under my kitchen sink. After I'd made a frantic search of both floors, she finally had pity on me and meowed, giving away her location. I found her curled up next to my housecleaning products. Thankfully, she hadn't sampled any.

By the time Saturday rolled around, I was ready for a break. It was my day off, so I decided it was high time my kitty bodyguard dog and I got out of the house. I looked forward to walking over to the fairground so we could check out the annual Fall Giant Flea Market & Antique Show.

Stormy started racing around and meowing when she saw me leashing Coal, so I picked her up and petted her thoroughly, hoping to calm her down. When that didn't work, I pulled out a package of kitty jingle balls I'd picked up from the dollar store. After throwing a couple down and hoping for the best, I took Coal outside and locked the door.

I stood on the porch a moment, catching my breath. "That cat's going to be the death of me," I said.

Coal whined and looked up at me. He didn't have far to look, since his head hit quite a bit above my waist. I gave him a reassuring ear scratch. "It's not your fault, boy. You're doing a great job watching her."

He trotted into the garden and went to the bathroom, then we headed out for our walk. The weather was what I'd consider perfect—I was able to wear long sleeves and jeans, but didn't need a jacket. I took my time ambling along, taking in the sights of town.

Blue skies contrasted with the hanging red begonias dotting the sidewalks, while slightly-browned hostas and ferns held onto summer in well-kept front yards. Everything felt idyllic, and I mentally scolded myself for giving in to my uneasy feelings earlier in the week. I loved living in Lewisburg, I loved my job, and I loved my dog. Of all the places I'd lived, which admittedly hadn't been many, West Virginia was the only place with a climate where I felt like I could actually breathe the air I was meant to breathe.

The flea market was hopping by the time we got there. I meandered around the display tables and considered buying another quilt, although I already had too many. I also found a red Fiestaware pitcher that was a perfect match to the dishes Bo had inherited from Auntie A, but I knew he wouldn't see the need for one, cute as it was.

I reached the edge of the tables and rounded a corner, coming up short when I realized who was running the weapons table so neatly laid out in front of me.

Kylie, my heavily tattooed barista, met my eyes and gave a slow smile. "So you're out and about today?" She looked down at Coal, her voice softening. "And you brought your big boy." Coal tugged at the leash and headed over to Kylie's outstretched hand, nearly knocking a knife off the table in the process. I steadied it as he accepted a chin scratch.

"What a great booth," I said, scanning the table. Kylie seemed to have everything, from muzzle loaders to Civil War-era swords to very modern knives. "I didn't know you sold these things."

She gave a brief nod, her dark bob swinging against her thin cheeks. The dragon tattoo that swirled up her neck and down her arms was almost fully visible under her short-sleeved black T-shirt. She wore her typical bright eyeshadow colors and heavy eyeliner. "Yeah, I've always been fascinated with weapons, and I've taught myself quite a bit about them.

I only acquire top quality stuff." She picked up a longer tarnished sword with an open basket-type hilt, holding it flat across her palms. "For instance, look at this sword. It's a Scottish backsword, and it cost me a pretty penny." She set it down, picking up a beautiful long knife. "And this is a hand-forged replica of a Viking seax. Look at the etched bone handle." I'd rarely seen my serious barista get so excited about something other than her foam art latte designs.

"That's gorgeous," I breathed. I had a feeling Bo would love it if I got him a gift like that.

Kylie gingerly picked up another knife and extended it toward me, hilt down. "Now this is a genuine Civil War era Bowie knife. One of my favorites."

I touched the knife, wondering what kinds of battles it had seen. "Kylie, this is a great hobby. I had no idea you were so knowledgeable."

She shrugged, and I knew her walls had gone up again. Kylie was what Auntie A would've called "a tough nut to crack."

Before she could comment, a blond, curly-haired guy in glasses strode up. He was in his twenties like Kylie. I tugged Coal back to my side and told him to sit.

"Hey," Kylie said quietly.

The guy glanced at Coal and me, but it was clear his entire focus was on Kylie. "Hey. I was just texting with Sparrow, and she said she got the chainmail in."

"That's good news. I know she was waiting on it a while." Kylie turned to me. "This is my friend Joel Fuller. We did Ren Faire together for a few years. Joel, this is one of my bosses at the cafe, Macy Hatfield."

I shook his hand, pleased to find he had a firm grip. That always spoke well for a man, and this particular man seemed to harbor a lot of interest in Kylie. Given the blasé look on Kylie's face, though, it was anyone's guess if the feeling was mutual.

I grinned at Joel. "Nice to meet you." Hoping to give Kylie more time with her friend, I said, "Well, I think Coal and I will mosey on along. I might drop by later."

We walked along the grass toward another booth that caught my eye. The table featured delicate hand-carved wooden objects. Smiling at the woman, who seemed a little leery of Coal, I stood back and admired the work. When I noticed one particular object, I couldn't stop myself from reaching down to examine it.

It was a wild and flowing waterfall. In an instant, I was dragged into the horror of my own story, reminded of how my parents had died in a sudden creek flood. Dad had managed to get Bo and me to higher ground, but when he'd gone back to get my mom, a mudslide trapped them in the house, which in turn collapsed. As we looked back at the facts, it seemed an unbelievable series of events. Only Bo was old enough to remember any of it, but he'd told me the story so many times, it was easy to see it play out in my mind.

"Were you interested in that one, hon?" The woman's soft voice pulled me back to the present. "It's made of box elder wood. My husband is a skilled craftsman. He spends all his free time carving away."

I yanked my hand back as if it had been burned. "Oh, no. I mean, it's lovely, but I can't buy it."

All my manners had flown out the window, and I felt like I couldn't even string sentences together. Tossing out a haphazard "thanks," I darted off toward other booths in an attempt to cover my awkward behavior. Coal stayed close to my side as if he picked up on my unease.

An art booth was set up nearby. I would have recognized it as Dylan's, even without seeing the table banner that featured the name of his gallery, The Discerning Palette. Dylan had a unique—and very well-honed—aesthetic when it came to artwork. Bo had hired him to decorate the cafe, and his art print choices had set the perfect tone.

He was leaning down, arranging something under the table. I cleared my throat and he stood, his dark blue eyes meeting my own. "Macy! How great to see you." A hesitant note crept into his voice. "And you, too, Coal."

Dogs weren't Dylan's thing—he'd told me he liked cats best. He swore he wasn't intimidated by Coal, but every time he ran into him, his voice took on that slightly nervous tone I was sure any dog would recognize.

Coal sat down and wagged his tail. He started panting, and I realized he was getting too hot in the increasing glare of the sun. I pulled him closer to where I was standing, under the white tent canopy.

Dylan, who was looking artsy as usual in black-framed glasses, a button-up shirt, and a lightweight scarf, gestured to an oversized black and white portrait at the front of the table that my eyes had returned to more than once. It featured a woman with an elongated neck and a cowboy hat. She had a challenging "come at me, bro" look in her eyes.

"I just got this one," he said. "I found this kid who dropped out of college and was hawking his wares on the street in D.C. I snapped up quite a few of his portraits, and I have a feeling he's going places fast."

I nodded, taking in the perfect shading and details. "Good eye." As Coal's panting intensified, I said, "I'd better go find some water for him."

"The concessions area is over to the left, by the antique

cars." Dylan rearranged a small oil painting, his long, tan fingers drawing my attention. The man had really nice hands. He glanced up from under his long eyelashes. "I haven't seen you for awhile, and I'd love to catch up. Would you want to join me for dinner tonight? Maybe hit the fusion restaurant you like?"

From his slightly disheveled brown bangs to his old school Hollywood cleft chin, Dylan had an allure that was hard to resist. On top of that, he seemed really interested in pursuing me, which was more than I could say about Titan McCoy.

"Sure," I said, looking forward to another interesting discussion with him. "What time?"

He grinned. "I'll pick you up around six, if that works."

"Sounds good." I gave Coal's leash a light tug. "Let's get you something to drink, boy."

After buying four water bottles, I picked up a big Tupperware bowl at a booth. I dumped the water into the bowl, watching as Coal greedily lapped up every last drop. I should've thought ahead and packed water for him, knowing how much Danes could guzzle.

I decided to blitz through the antique car show area before heading home. On our way there, as I dodged into a space between booths, some guy in a dark hoodie came barreling toward me. I tried to sidestep him, but he still brushed into me. Coal gave a low growl. I turned to watch the rude man's back as he charged toward the flea market entrance. Something was definitely off about him—no one was wearing a hot sweatshirt in this weather.

Kylie wasn't at her booth as I passed it. Instead, Joel sat in her place, watching over her weapons. I nodded at him, making a mental note to drop by on my way out. I wanted to get that Viking seax for Bo before someone else snagged it.

The antique car section wasn't busy at all, but I did bump into Doctor Stan Stokes, the family practice doctor who'd treated us as kids. He was retired now, and I was glad to see that he was enjoying his free time. I was fairly certain he owned one of the antique cars—probably the dark blue Ford convertible he was standing next to.

"Macy, how good to see you," he said. "And look at your doggie! How sleek he is. Would he let me pet him?"

Given the fact that the doctor *wanted* to pet Coal, I didn't figure it would be a problem. I walked Coal closer, allowing the doctor to lean down and give him a few head pats in his fatherly way. Despite the fact that I'd dreaded shots at Doctor Stokes' office, I'd always appreciated his kind and listening manner.

He straightened. "What a good dog. You two enjoy the car show. There are some real beauts along the side there." He pointed off to the right.

I nodded, heading in that direction. Coal began to whine, which was odd. Maybe he wanted to return to the doctor? Or maybe he was getting hot again? I stopped and looked at him. He wasn't panting.

I decided to walk a little farther, then get home. I checked out a green truck and a silver roadster, but Coal seemed to become increasingly anxious. He started pulling me toward the last car in the lineup—a dark red Buick sedan. He sniffed at the ground near the back door of the vehicle, then gave several urgent yips.

"What's gotten into you, boy?" I asked, peering into the front seat. The pristine white leather interior was obviously a custom job. My gaze wandered to the back seat, where I caught sight of something lying on the back floor.

The moment I figured out what I was looking at, I froze. It was a *person*. And that person was most likely dead, because he was lying flat on his face, with a sword protruding from a bloody wound in his back.

4

Coal chose this exact moment to give voice to a single, booming bark. I literally jumped.

"Shh, knock it off!" I hissed. I needed to clear my head and think. But as I glanced at the prostrate form one more time, I knew I didn't possess any measure of chill.

Turning, I took off in the general direction of Doctor Stokes. I started flailing my arms like a crazy person. He caught sight of me and rushed over. "What's going on?"

I couldn't even articulate what I'd seen. I simply took hold of his arm and pulled him toward the red car. "In the back," I managed, pointing a shaky finger that way. I pulled to a complete stop about twelve feet away, knowing Coal didn't need to get anywhere near the corpse.

The doctor peered inside, then tried the doors. "All locked," he said. "But given the amount of blood under him and the fact I can't see any movement, he must be dead." His white brows were drawn together in bewilderment.

I felt equally dumbfounded. Who would stab someone in the back at a flea market, then dump him into an antique car where he'd be sure to be found? I managed to gather my wits. "Okay. I'll call 9-1-1."

As I did so, the doctor stood guard over the vehicle. Once I hung up, Coal pulled at his leash, trying to get closer to the strange smells he knew weren't right.

"I need to get him out of here," I said. "Would you mind staying with...with the body?" Because yes, we were indeed living in the bizarre world where I was discussing a corpse with my family doctor.

"Of course." Doctor Stokes placed a steadying hand on my arm. "But I'm sure the police will need to talk with you, so you really shouldn't go far."

I nodded. "Right. I'll be over at the weapons booth. My barista runs it."

And then it hit me. Kylie ran a booth full of weapons. The dead man was obviously killed with a sword.

Suddenly, my premonition was starting to make a whole lot of sense.

As I APPROACHED Kylie's booth, I was relieved to see her standing there, deep in conversation with Joel. She threw a glance my way, then did a double take.

"Miss Hatfield, are you okay?" She rushed over to my side. She'd used my formal name, which we'd asked our employees to call us in public, but somehow it felt wrong today. "You look so pale."

In the hubbub of calling for help, I'd forgotten that my typical reaction to blood was to feel faint. It must be catching up with me now.

"Maybe I'll just sit down," I said, making a move toward the ground.

Kylie pulled me up, gesturing toward her chair. "No, please, sit here."

With Kylie's hand under my arm and Joel's arm around me, I made my way to the chair and sank into it. Coal positioned himself by my side.

"What happened?" Kylie's voice was worried. "Is something wrong with Bo—I mean, Mr. Hatfield?"

I gave a quick shake of my head, aware that Kylie and my brother shared a special bond. It was not at all romantic, but more of an unspoken, respectful recognition between two people who had seen the darkest sides of life and still managed to emerge victorious. Although Kylie had never opened up about what she'd been through, her tattoos, clothing, and attitude—not to mention her apparent fascination with weapons—gave clear warnings to all who tried to get close.

My voice came out scratchy. "No. It was over there with the antique cars. I found—I mean *Coal* found—a dead body."

"What?" Joel's face was perplexed. "You mean for real?"

I nodded. "This was no joke. Someone stabbed a guy with a sword and he was lying face-down in one of those cars. Doctor Stokes is over there now, waiting for the police to come."

Joel took one long look at me, then turned to Kylie. "You stay with her—she might need some water. I'll go over and help the doctor protect the car from any gawkers."

I appreciated Joel's get-'er-done attitude, which reminded me of Bo. Kylie nodded, pulling a ginger ale from a cooler under the table and cracking the lid. She passed it to me. "Here, sip on this."

I did as instructed and felt better. As long as I didn't think about the blood...

"What did he look like?" Kylie asked.

I tried to think beyond the sword in the back. "Given what he was wearing and his build, I think he was a younger man, like in his twenties or thirties. I think he had a dark beard, although I couldn't see much of his face because it was toward the floor."

Kylie's face did a rapid shift from mild curiosity to real concern. She said, "Hang on, I have to talk to Joel a sec," and speed-walked off toward the antique cars.

I took another sip of ginger ale, then leaned forward to see what Kylie was doing. Coal helpfully scooched a little closer to me, offering his head and neck for support, so I gladly draped myself against his sturdy frame as I spied on my barista.

Kylie stalked up to the red Buick without saying a word to Joel and the doctor, who were standing off to the side of the car, chatting. She peered into the back window and seemed to stiffen. Then she wheeled around, pulling her phone from her pocket and heading toward the concession area.

That girl was an enigma wrapped in a mystery with a side of conundrum. Had she recognized the victim? And if she had, why didn't she stop to tell the doctor and Joel who he was?

By the time police officers strode toward Joel and the doctor, Kylie had moved well out of my view. I was relieved to see that our detective friend, Charlie Hatcher, was on the scene. Doctor Stokes talked to him for a few minutes, then he pointed my way. Detective Hatcher nodded and walked toward Kylie's booth.

Detective Hatcher was youthful looking man in his fifties with steely gray hair and a dimpled cheek. I'd known him long enough to understand that his calm demeanor and cute dimple were misleading. He was serious about catching criminals, and, thanks to Bo's DEA connections, he was always open to working with us when gathering information.

"Macy." He smiled my way, then stopped to give Coal an ear scratch. Taking out a pen and small notebook, he said, "Why don't you tell me what happened over there, if you don't mind."

I told him everything. When I finished, he looked at Coal. "So your dog sniffed the body out, did he? Good boy." His eyes met and held mine. "And you're saying the sword was protruding from the man's back when you found him?"

A wave of nausea threatened to sweep over me. "Yes, it was."

His gaze dropped to Kylie's display table and he took a step closer, examining the weapons. He picked up a sword that resembled the one in the dead man's back. After touching the metal hilt, he lightly ran a finger along the point, which looked fairly sharp.

His gaze darkened, just enough to jolt me with the realization that he was mulling over a theory I wasn't going to care for. His question confirmed the direction of his thoughts.

"Is there a reason you're resting at this *particular* booth, Macy? I believe it's the only weapons display here today."

I scrambled to explain. "Well, yes. This is my barista's booth. She's one of our best employees. She does the latte foam art, you know? She's a fan favorite over at Barks & Beans." I was over-explaining, a habit that always kicked in when I felt like I was on the spot. "She's great," I added lamely.

Detective Hatcher nodded like I was making complete sense. "And what's her name?" he prodded.

"Kylie Baer," I said, hoping I wasn't throwing my barista under the bus.

Joel came over and joined us. "Kylie's a good friend of mine," he said.

"And where would Kylie be right now?" the detective asked.

I shot Joel a glance, unsure just how close he and Kylie were. I spoke up before he could. "She's on the phone, probably still on the fairgrounds." At least I hoped she was.

"Okay." The detective shoved the notepad back in his pocket. Gesturing to Joel, he said, "And you've already given one of my officers your account of things?"

Joel nodded. "Yes, sir."

Detective Hatcher looked at me. "Would you mind giving your barista a text or call and asking her to return to the scene? I need to head back over there, but I'm anxious to speak with her."

I knew that was code for, "Get Kylie back over here now." I slipped my phone from my pocket. "I'll text her," I assured him.

Giving us both a brief nod, the detective walked off toward the antique cars. I texted Kylie that she needed to come back to her booth because the police were here. As I waited for a response, I stood up to stretch. Coal jumped to his feet next to me, waiting for my next move. He'd started panting again. "You ready to get home, boy?" I asked, hoping Joel would volunteer to watch Kylie's booth again.

Joel's nervous blue eyes met mine. "I wasn't planning to

stay here this long. I need to get going soon, since I have a pretty long drive ahead of me. Do you think we need to pack up her table?"

"No need to do that." Although somewhat deflated that I'd have to stick around, I tried to sound cheery. "You feel free to go—I'll wait here for Kylie. I'm sure she'll be back soon." At least I hoped so.

Joel still seemed apprehensive. "I hate to leave without saying goodbye. I'd hoped that I'd have a little more time with her."

I took a good, long look at the clean-cut guy standing next to me, nary a visible tattoo on his body. I was a little surprised that he was Kylie's type. But there was an earnestness about him she might find endearing. She'd never mentioned having a boyfriend, but then again, she never mentioned anything personal to me.

"So you and Kylie go way back?" I asked, curious as to the nature of their relationship.

He tilted his head. "Well, just over the past few years. I joust at the Ren Faire and she runs her weapons booth there." His eyes brightened. "This year, I'm actually trying to talk her into doing some jousting with me. She's a natural on a horse. But I'm not sure she'll even be able to attend, now that her younger sister is moved in with her."

"Is her sister giving her a hard time?" Just last month, Kylie had come to work looking disheveled, and when I'd asked, she said something about her sister staying out too late. I'd hoped things had calmed down for her.

Joel's lips twisted. "Chelsea is a troublemaker, and she always had been. Kylie was actually my girlfriend a couple of years ago, but then Chelsea came along and busted everything up. She told Kylie a pack of lies about me coming onto her. Kylie dumped me like a hot potato, and I've been trying to convince her that Chelsea was lying ever since."

That would explain Kylie's nonchalant attitude toward him.

"I think Kylie's overwhelmed trying to keep tabs on Chelsea," he added. "She's only twenty, but she's a handful."

"But where are her parents?" I asked. "Why isn't Chelsea staying with them?"

He shrugged. "Kylie's really closed-lipped about her parents. All I know is that they don't seem to want anything to do with either of their daughters. Kylie moved out at nineteen." He glanced at his phone. "I really should get back. I drove up from Raleigh so I could see Kylie today, but I have work I need to get done this weekend. I already gave the cops my card and phone number if they need to ask me anything else." He adjusted his glasses and gave me a small smile. "Please let Kylie know I said goodbye."

"Will do. Nice to meet you, Joel."

As he walked away, I reluctantly sat back down. An older man hesitated as he noticed the weapons on Kylie's table, but the moment his gaze traveled to Coal, he hurried away. I hoped Kylie would return soon, before my intimidating dog started deterring her customers.

My phone buzzed and I grabbed it, relieved to see it was Kylie on the other end. "Where are you?" I asked.

She sounded out of breath. "I'm on my way—I'll be there in five. Did Joel leave?"

"Yeah, he said he had to get back to North Carolina," I said. "He's already talked to the police."

"Okay. Well, I'll be over there soon." I couldn't tell if she felt disappointed about missing Joel's departure. "Would you mind staying at my booth a little longer?"

I looked at Coal, who licked his lips. I'd have to get him more water before we walked home. But Kylie needed me. "Sure," I said.

"Thanks," she said.

Hanging up, I looked over at Detective Hatcher. He was deep in conversation with a gloved officer who was holding the offending sword in a bag. The detective wore an intense look, like he meant business.

I had a feeling Kylie was about to head straight into the lion's den, and I only hoped she had a really good explanation as to why she'd walked away from a murder scene.

5

COAL HAD SETTLED on the ground and was trying to go to sleep when Kylie finally walked up. After giving me a serious nod, she headed straight over to the police officers, who were still milling around the taped-off scene.

Detective Hatcher motioned her toward him, and I sat still for a few moments, trying to listen in. It was an exercise in futility, thanks to the birds that were sitting atop a nearby building, merrily chirping their heads off.

I couldn't let Kylie face the firing squad alone. "C'mon, boy," I whispered, giving Coal a nudge. "Let's go see Kylie." He recognized her name and perked up, leading me toward her.

The police had already removed the man's covered body, so at least Coal wouldn't get distracted trying to sniff the corpse. Maybe Detective Hatcher wouldn't want me lurking around, but I'd stay as unobtrusive as possible and try to put in a good word here and there for Kylie.

The detective was holding up the clear evidence bag with the sword in it, and to my dismay, Kylie was giving a slow nod. "Yes, that's one of mine," she said, her voice remarkably composed. "It was on my table this morning."

"Did you leave the table at any time?" the detective asked.

"I did." Kylie's back was rigid and her chin high, as if daring the detective to accuse her of something. "I went to the bathroom a couple of times, but my neighbor watched my booth for me. Then there were a few times I had to get weapons out of my bins and things, so my eyes weren't on it constantly."

She didn't mention the longer stretch of time when she'd left Joel in charge, but I sensed she might be trying to keep him out of the story. If I butted in to share that fact right now, it would look like I was going against her. After all, she *had* told the truth by saying she hadn't constantly been vigilant, I supposed.

It certainly looked like someone had swiped a sword right out from under her.

I tried to take Kylie's measure from Detective Hatcher's point of view. Her well-worn combat boots were positioned wide apart, like she was ready to pounce on someone if they came for her. Her glittery eyeshadow highlighted the sparks in her hazel eyes, and her black T-shirt read "Savage." If first impressions were everything, Kylie definitely knew how to make one.

The detective began flipping through his notebook pages, occasionally giving voice to a thoughtful murmur. Kylie shifted on her feet, visibly unnerved—which might have been the desired effect.

Finally, Detective Hatcher stabbed at a page in his notebook. "Now, Joel stated that you came over and looked into the car while he and the doctor were standing watch over the victim. He said you walked off quickly, visibly upset." He waited just a beat, then asked, "Did you recognize the victim, Miss Baer?"

Kylie's face blanched, and I had the distinct impression she was considering lying. "I did," she said finally, apparently committing to the truth. "He's a guy my sister was seeing— Alec Marchand. He's originally from France, but just became a U.S. citizen this year." She clammed up.

The detective seemed to soften as he recognized the distaste in her tone. "And what was your impression of Marchand?" he pressed.

Kylie frowned. "He was a player and a user, and I mean a *drug* user, too," she says. "I wanted my sister to walk away from him, but she wouldn't listen. It's not the first bad relationship she's jumped into headfirst."

"So you didn't want to see your sister in this relationship and you urged her to get out of it." Detective Hatcher threw a thoughtful look my way. His smooth voice was filled with understanding. "That reminds me of Macy, there—she and her brother always have each other's backs, just like you and your sister. They'd do anything for each other."

I had the distinct feeling that the detective was trying to break down Kylie's defenses and lead her into a trap. I tried to shoot her a warning look, but it was too late.

She nodded vigorously. "Exactly. It's my job to look out for my kid sister, even though she is twenty years old." She glanced thoughtfully at the Buick. Under her breath, she added, "My parents certainly aren't going to."

Detective Hatcher slid his notebook into his pocket. "Of course. Thank you for answering my questions. Would you mind hanging around until we can go down to the station and talk a little more, Miss Baer? I'll probably leave in about thirty minutes or so. I'll need to speak with your sister, as well."

I decided to throw in my two cents' worth. "Kylie is on duty at the cafe on Monday," I said, leveling a gaze at the detective. "I'd hate for anything to interfere with her work duties."

He smiled, but it wasn't his most friendly smile. "We won't be keeping her long, I'm sure." He turned back to his men.

Kylie looked worried. "Did I say something wrong, do you think?"

I tried to reassure her, even though I had a feeling the detective had gone fishing for a motive and might have hooked one. "I'm sure you were fine. You might want to go over and pack up your table, so you'll be ready to go back to the station with him." Coal's panting had grown louder, and I placed a calming hand on his big head. "I really need to get him home now," I said. "Will your sister be able to get down to the station on her own?"

To my surprise, Kylie's eyes and nose reddened, like she was about to cry. "Oh, no! She usually borrows my car to get anywhere." She threw a backward glance at the detective. "Do you think he'll let me drive myself to the station? Or maybe he'd stop to pick her up?"

I met Kylie's wild gaze. "Listen, don't worry about a thing. Just let your sister know I'll pick her up in about forty minutes or so. That way you can focus on packing up."

Relief filled her voice. "Okay. Thank you so much." She gave me her address, then said, "I'll call and let her know when you'll be there."

As Coal and I trudged off to grab some more water before heading home, I considered the unfamiliar, vulnerable side of Kylie I'd seen today. She was ready to take the fall for her sister, and maybe even for her old boyfriend. She had a soft heart beating under that unsociable exterior, and despite the tragic circumstances of the day, I was glad I'd finally gotten a glimpse of it.

AFTER GUZZLING two huge bowls of water and nibbling at his food, Coal lumbered over to his bed in the living room. He kneaded the supersized pillow exactly three times, which was his routine before dropping off to sleep. Although Stormy started frisking around him, even going so far as to pounce on his extended paws, Coal merely gave her a weary look before closing his eyes.

I threw a load of laundry in the wash, then used my cold brewed coffee and cream to make an iced coffee drink before heading out to pick up Chelsea. I wondered how Kylie was doing. Hopefully this whole thing would blow over for her, but given that it was her sword stuck in the body, it seemed unlikely she'd be exonerated quickly. And it couldn't be a coincidence that Chelsea happened to be dating the dead guy.

After grabbing my keys and giving both Coal and Stormy pats on the head, I walked out to my compact SUV. I plugged Kylie's directions into my phone and pulled onto the main road, glancing at the cafe as I drove by. It seemed to be busy, with several people enjoying our outdoor seating. Bo would be happy to know things were humming along as usual in his absence.

Kylie's house turned out to be a quaint, moss-green cottage. I walked up the shrub-lined brick walk and knocked on the navy door, which already sported a black and orange Halloween wreath.

The door cracked open and a girl who looked to be about sixteen peered out. She had long, white-blonde hair and heavy black eyeliner.

I smiled. "Hi, I'm—"

She interrupted. "Macy, I know. Kylie told me. Hang on." She disappeared into the house, returning with a small black backpack in hand. "Okay, we can go," she said, stepping out and slamming the door behind her.

"Uh, don't you have to lock it?" I asked.

"It locks automatically," she said, pointing to a keypad I hadn't noticed before. She gave me a disgruntled huff.

I felt utterly chastised for my mom-like admonition. I also felt about a hundred years old with this cheeky young sprig beside me. It was getting easier to understand how this kid could drive her sister nuts.

Determined to be friendly, I opened the passenger door for Chelsea, who rewarded me with a skeptical look. She wore a black velvet choker on her neck, and although her clothing was relatively plain, she had at least ten piercings in each ear. Her style could be summed up as "babe in the wood meets Goth"—she was innocent and dangerous, all wrapped up in one. I supposed that look would be highly attractive to a man like Alec, at least the way Kylie described him.

As I drove toward the station, I said, "Kylie told you what happened?"

"Barely," she said, snapping her gum. "I mean, she told me my boyfriend got stabbed."

I glanced over, surprised at her upbeat demeanor. I would've expected at least some measure of grief, but then again, Chelsea seemed to be the type who reveled in breaking every expectation placed on her.

Trying to steer the conversation—one-sided as it was—onto safer ground, I said, "Your sister does such a great job at the cafe. We're so pleased to have her. She's really talented."

Instead of responding, Chelsea looked at me like I was an alien.

I decided that at thirty-eight, I was apparently over the hill and therefore not qualified to conduct any kind of discussion with Chelsea. Falling silent, I drove her up to the police station door, where Kylie was waiting outside. She raced down the steps to meet us.

Compared to her sister, I realized that Kylie was actually quite friendly.

"Thanks so much, Miss Hatfield," she said. Her eyeshadow had faded, like she'd been rubbing her eyes. "The detective let me bring my car, so I'll be able to take us home." She looked at Chelsea. "You ready to go in?" she asked.

"How come?" Chelsea said jauntily. "Didn't you already identify the body?"

I couldn't take another moment of the insolence. "I'd better be going," I said. "Let me know if you need anything else, Kylie."

She nodded her dark head before leading her flippant sister up the stairs. I actually felt bad for Detective Hatcher as he'd be the one to try to get answers out of Chelsea.

Kylie had her hands full in more ways than one. I wondered if she had any kind of support system, especially if her parents were as uninvolved as Joel had said. Once again, I felt the need to befriend our barista, but I knew the only way she'd open up to me would be on her own time and in her own way.

6

Coal met me at the back door, his eyes anxious. I stepped into the house and looked around, wondering why he was upset. Stormy sat on her perch, cleaning her back. But something smelled...wet. Like laundry detergent, I realized.

Rushing toward the laundry room, I stepped into a puddle of bubbly water that was rapidly spreading across the floor. With a flying leap, I jumped toward the washing machine and shut it off.

Fury rose in me as I saw that the protective cardboard boxes I'd stretched over the backs of the machines had been knocked to the floor and were now sopping wet. Also, the drain hose connecting the washer to the drainpipe had been bumped out, thus dumping water all over the floor.

I knew exactly who had done this, and it wasn't Coal, who was standing in the laundry room door, ready to come to my assistance if needed.

Trying to calm my temper, I unplugged both the washer and the dryer. Easing back into the water, I splashed toward the bathroom to grab towels.

"You'd better be glad I came back when I did," I yelled in the general direction of the cat. "You could've flooded my whole downstairs, you toot!"

Knowing that my ire was directed toward Stormy, Coal glanced at the living room like he was asking if I'd give him permission to rough the kitty up a bit.

I scratched behind his ear and tried to calm down. "Not now, boy. It'll be okay. It's going to be okay." I stomped back into the laundry room, tossing nearly all my clean towels on top of the frothy mess.

A knock sounded at my back door, so I glanced down before going to see who it was. My jeans were wet up to my knees, my dirty shirt was half-tucked, and I was fairly certain I'd smeared bubbles into my hair. There was no way I could make myself look presentable. "Coming," I shouted, making my way over.

Vera stood outside, a covered Pyrex dish in hand. "Hey there, I remembered you liked my Tuscan chicken casserole, and once again, I've made too much. It's warm," she added.

"Thanks so much," I said, taking the proffered dish. As my stomach growled, I realized it was long past lunchtime and I was starving.

Vera glanced down at my jeans. "Everything okay?"

Nope—everything was falling apart without Bo around to keep an eye on his wildcat. I forced a smile. "It's under control now. I just had a little washing machine accident." I shot a glare at Stormy, who turned her back to me and started scratching the living tar out of her carpeted perch.

Vera followed my irritated gaze. "I see," she said. "Well, I know some good repairmen if you need anyone."

"Thanks so much for the casserole," I said. "You're a lifesaver."

She smiled before walking down the steps. I shut the door and hustled into the kitchen, grabbing a fork and sinking it into the savory casserole without even bothering to dish it up first. I waved my fork at Stormy. "I hope you're feeling proud of yourself," I said. "Because I'm going to tell your dad everything you did to me."

Another knock sounded on the door. I opened it to see Vera standing there again.

"Oh, hi," I said.

She gestured toward my garden fence, her brow wrinkled. "There's a man standing out on the sidewalk, and he said he's looking for you," she said. "I told him I'd let you know." She leaned in, cupping her mouth as she spoke. "I wasn't sure if he was on the up-and-up."

I followed her down the stairs and over to the gate. The blond man who turned to say hello was the very last person on earth I'd expected to see today—or ever. I gripped the fencepost as his eyes met mine.

Hazel-green eyes tucked under honey-colored eyelashes. A haircut and face that looked straight out of a cologne ad. A knowing smile that had once been reserved only for me.

Jake Hollings, my ex-husband, had come to town.

I couldn't say a word. It was like we'd fallen into a time warp where I was forced to stand and behold his beauty.

Vera placed an encouraging hand on my arm, breaking my silence.

"Vera," I choked out, "This is my husband—my *ex*-husband—Jake. Jake, this is my neighbor, Vera."

True to form, Jake flashed a brilliant smile at her. "I'm mighty pleased to meet you, Miss Vera." His southern accent was understated, but alluring.

Vera blinked and returned the greeting, only far less

enthusiastically. "I'll be scooting on along now, Macy," she said. Her dark eyes sparked with an unspoken loyalty. "Call me if you need anything, hon," she added, brushing past Jake on her way up the sidewalk.

Unfazed by the older woman's aloofness, Jake turned his full powers of radiance upon me. "It's sure been a long time," he said, his voice deep. He stepped through the gate and wrapped me in a hug before I could refuse. My still-wet shirt pressed against him, and I felt like a total mess.

I shook my head in an attempt to clear my thinking. "That's not because of me, Jake. You were the one who torpedoed our marriage and walked out, as you might recall." I needed to extricate myself from his magnetic web.

My words bounced off him like balloons off a dartboard. "I had some news to share," he said. "Would you mind if we sat down somewhere?"

I knew he was inviting himself into my house, but there was no way that was happening, even though it was now at least seventy-five degrees in the shade. "Sure, have a seat on my porch," I said, feeling like I'd just invited the devil to dance.

I plopped into a chair without waiting for him to sit. He followed suit, then wiped at the sheen of sweat on his forehead. "I forgot to bring my water bottle," he said. "Would you mind getting me something to drink?"

So my ex was now sitting on *my* porch, asking that I serve him? That was rich. My head was getting clearer and clearer by the minute.

I opened the wooden back door and stalked into the kitchen, slamming open the cupboard and pulling out a chipped glass. Coal had positioned himself near the door, his head cocked, and I knew he was monitoring the tone of our conversation. He wanted to know what kind of man was sitting on my porch, and I had half a mind to let him find out.

I poured water in, because I wasn't about to share my sweet tea with Jake. He'd always been crazy about my special brew, which required a specific brand of teabag and a copious amount of sugar. He wasn't worthy of it now.

I headed through the back door, but decided to leave it open, with just the screen door between us. That way Coal could keep an eye on things—a rather threatening eye.

As I handed the glass to Jake, a low growl sounded from inside. Jake whipped his head toward the door, his eyes widening.

"What's that? Did you get a dog?" he asked.

"You shouldn't be surprised," I said, shrugging. "You always knew I loved dogs. I just couldn't have one in our rental place."

He peered at Coal's shadowy figure looming behind the screen. "That's a big dog," he said.

Coal gave a prolonged yowl, followed by a short bark.

"He is indeed," I said calmly. "Now, what did you come all the way from South Carolina to tell me?" I couldn't imagine what would've warranted such a long trip, and I feared the worst.

"My dad's retiring by the end of the year," Jake said, sipping at his water. "He's leaving the car dealership to me."

I wasn't sure what he was angling at, so I gave a knowing nod. "Good for you." Jake had always dreamed of moving up in the world, and I guessed he must see this as his opportunity to do so.

"I'm excited about it," he continued. Those entrancing eyes fixed on mine, looking more green than gold in the shade. "Hey, I checked out your cafe as I drove by—what a great place! You really did it up right. I've been following any mentions of it online, and I saw that your one-year anniversary is coming up. You should be proud of the business you've built here."

"Well, Bo's really the mastermind behind things," I said, watching as Jake's lip curled slightly in distaste. Jake had never liked Bo.

He leaned in. "You're just being modest. I've always been impressed with your brains, among other things." His tone turned more intimate and his gaze caressed my face. "You look healthy here," he said. "You're practically glowing, and your hair's so long and wild."

Everything about me was wild today thanks to the washing machine debacle, but he didn't seem to notice my dirty clothing.

Coal gave another growl, this time much closer. He'd pressed his black nose into the screen, and his teeth were visible.

"He's not very friendly, is he?" Jake sounded personally affronted.

"He's a good judge of character," I retorted.

Jake finally seemed to pick up on my distaste. He set his glass down on the side table. "Listen, I won't keep you, but I wanted to tell you personally that things are over with Sherry Dunford. She doesn't work at the dealership anymore."

Sherry was the receptionist Jake had cheated on me with. Well, Sherry, among others.

"Okay," I said, still uncertain what response he was looking for. A high five?

He scooted to the edge of his seat, allowing his knee to rest against mine. "I wanted to apologize to you, Macy," he said. "I know I've hurt you, time and time again. I want to make amends."

I withdrew into my chair, unwilling to maintain physical contact with this man who'd almost managed to crush my spirit completely. "There's no need for that," I said. "I wasn't keeping score. You had affairs, you lied to me, you ended our marriage. That was the end of it."

His look turned beseeching. "I'll be in town for a few days—over at the hotel by the river. Maybe we could meet up sometime and visit that hole-in-the-wall Mexican place we ate at a couple years ago."

I stiffened. It was high time to shut this unplanned reunion down. "No. We won't be meeting up, Jake. I'm really busy right now with the cafe. Bo's out of town, so I have even more responsibility than usual. Plus, we're having some...employee issues. I don't have any energy to spare."

He frowned, then started to stand. I jumped to my feet before he did, unwilling to let him make me feel smaller in any way. He stretched his arms out, and as I drew back to avoid another hug, Coal bashed the door open. I grabbed his collar as he lunged for my ex, who skipped the steps entirely and toppled onto the ground below.

Jake scrambled to his feet and dusted off his jeans. I gripped Coal's collar tighter, sending the message he wasn't to budge.

"That dog is a horse." Jake was more ruffled than I'd ever seen him. His carefully combed blond bangs were in a disarray and his polo shirt was smudged with dirt.

It felt good having the upper hand for once. "Goodbye, Jake. Congrats on the dealership."

He gave a brisk nod. "If you decide you want to talk, you know my number. I'll be around." He strode out the gate.

That's what I was afraid of—that he would stick around. I didn't want to see or even think of him again. I'd started a new life here, and Jake wasn't a part of it.

Coal nuzzled his nose into my palm. "Good boy," I said. "Though you nearly scared me to death. What would you have done if I hadn't caught you?" I glanced at my phone, wishing I could touch base with Bo to tell him the crazy events of the day.

It was nearly five-thirty, and it suddenly hit me that Dylan was picking me up for a date at six. I'd completely forgotten. I was a total wreck, and there was no way I'd be ready in time. I reluctantly picked up the phone and called him.

"What's up?" he asked.

"I'm really sorry, but I don't think I can go out tonight— I've had some things come up," I said.

"Anything I can help you with?" he asked.

I considered. "I have a big mess in my laundry room right now, since Bo's cat knocked the drain pipe out. But I think I've got it under control."

I could hear the worry in Dylan's voice. "That doesn't sound good. Hey, what if I bring food to you? Then I could help you with the cleanup and we could just hang out a little."

Somehow I couldn't picture Dylan Butler getting his fine-looking hands dirty, but I was willing to give him a shot. "Sure. That would be great."

After agreeing he could come over at six-thirty, I hung up and called Kylie. She picked up quickly, which I hoped was a good sign.

"Hey, how are you?" I asked. "Are you and Chelsea home yet?"

"We are." She sounded relieved. "Chelsea didn't really have much information on Alec. I guess he hid a lot from her. *Quelle surprise.*"

I nearly toppled to the floor. "You know French?" I asked.

"*Mais oui,*" she said, offering no further explanation. "Anyway, thanks again for all your help today. I'll see you on Monday."

She hung up before I could say goodbye.

So much for my friendship goals. It sounded like Kylie didn't want any further help from me. I slogged into the still-wet laundry room, tossing a few dry towels onto the floor. Life had taught me one lesson I was pretty sure Kylie hadn't learned yet, and that was that sometimes, our messes got too big to clean up on our own. Sometimes we needed to reach out for help.

I resolved to be there for Kylie and Chelsea in spite of their fierce independence. Although Detective Hatcher had let them go, until Alec's murderer was caught, the sisters would remain persons of interest in the case. They were a long way from being completely off the hook.

7

AFTER STAYING up until midnight to chat about art and books with Dylan, I was dragging for church in the morning. Thankfully, although people still dressed up for the services, I didn't feel pressured to put on a full face of makeup. Summer showed up about five minutes early to pick me up, and we headed over together.

Bo's absence was palpable as we sang familiar hymns and listened to the sermon. Usually, we discussed key points on the way home, but Summer and I traveled back in silence. I knew she missed Bo as much as I did.

Finally, she said, "Did you see the news this morning?"

I knew Summer liked to keep her finger on the pulse of local events, in particular the lost dog and cat groups, just in case any of them showed up at her shelter.

"I didn't have time. I got up a little later."

She grinned. "Ah, you mentioned Dylan came over. Did you two get the laundry room back in order?"

I let out a groan. "Yes, but now I have to keep the door shut. I had to move Stormy's litter box to the bathroom."

Summer's nose crinkled. "I know what that means—litter underfoot."

"Exactly," I said. "Maybe next time Bo has to go out of town, you could keep Stormy. After all, you already have cats."

Summer gave a long blink. "We'll see. Anyway, like I was saying about the news—that guy you found dead turns out to have been a thief."

I twisted in my seat to stare at her. "What do you mean?"

"Just what I said. Apparently, he worked in the men's department over at the mall, and they caught him stealing high-end clothing and colognes. He'd recently been fired."

"I'm not surprised," I said grimly.

She pulled up to the curb by my house and unlocked the doors. "But you didn't know him, right?"

"No, but Kylie said he was a scoundrel—into drugs and other things. She was right."

Summer leaned back in her seat, turning her brown gaze on me. She'd arranged her dark honey-blonde hair in an intricate bun atop her head. She wasn't wearing a trace of makeup, so she looked like a throwback to her renounced Mennonite roots. "Do you think Kylie...I mean that guy *was* dating her younger sister. Could she—"

I stopped her in her tracks. "No way. Kylie would never do that."

Summer gave a slow nod. "Okay, sure. You know her better than I do." She thoughtfully twisted a piece of hair that had fallen out of her bun. "Still, I wouldn't want to tangle with her."

"Just because she looks dangerous doesn't mean she is," I said.

"I'm not talking about how she looks. I can sense she's

more...I don't know. She's more *jaded* than we are, Macy. I know you like to see the best in people, and I do, too. I'm just saying you should be a little wary with her."

"Well, Bo likes her," I retorted. "He's a good judge of character, and he certainly gives no one the benefit of the doubt."

"You're right about that," Summer said. "There's just something kind of wild and uncontrollable simmering beneath Kylie's surface. I've felt it when I'm around her." She slapped a hand to her leg. "Shoot, Macy, I can't really explain it. Just be careful."

Feeling strangely scolded, I nodded and opened my car door. "You want to come in and help me eat some leftover chicken casserole?"

Summer gave a reluctant shake of her head. "I can't. I got a text that Animal Control's bringing a couple of dogs over soon. I'll need to check them in."

"Okay. Thanks for driving me—and thanks for the warning. I'll keep it in mind," I said.

As Summer pulled out, I thought about what she'd said. I'd known my friend long enough to notice that her instinctual feelings about people usually turned out to be right. She picked up on things I didn't. I wished I could get Bo's take on Kylie, but it might be awhile before we talked again. My heart gave a sad lurch, knowing Bo was alone in dangerous territory. Sure, it wasn't his first time in a life-threatening situation, but back in his Marine and DEA days, I wasn't aware of what he was doing. Now I was, and knowing was the hardest part.

MONDAY WAS DRIZZLY AND OVERCAST, tempting me to wrap up in a quilt and stay home. Since that wasn't an option, I dragged myself up early to open the cafe. Kylie and Charity showed up to set up the cafe area, while Summer dropped off the shelter dogs of the day. One was a small Pomeranian mix, and the other was a thin brown mutt that looked like it had seen better days. "Sorry about that one," Summer said, gesturing to the forlorn dog. "I cleaned him up and I've fed him well, but he's still dragging around. The vet's going to check him over tomorrow. He's one of the ones Animal Control picked up over by the dump."

"I wonder if someone dropped him off there?" I asked.

Summer's lips twisted downward. "Wouldn't be the first time." She handed me the leashes. "If you don't mind, I'm going to grab my joe and get going. Just let me know if he has any issues."

"Will do," I said.

She leaned closer. "Remember what I said."

As she walked off, I glanced at Kylie, who seemed to be running full steam ahead this morning. She'd taken time to do her hair and makeup, so that boded well.

Vera stopped in around ten and picked up something from the cafe. With her take-out cup and bag in hand, she headed into the Barks section and had a seat. I held onto the Pomeranian, who wanted to go sniff her out—or maybe her food.

"I thought I'd try one of those chicken salad wraps and check out the doggies," she said. "I can't stay long since I have a book club meeting, but I wanted to ask how things went with your ex." Her concerned brown gaze held mine. "I remembered your great aunt didn't have much good to say about him."

I was surprised that Auntie A had even spoken to Vera about Jake, but it made sense because the two friends had been close. Vera hadn't moved back to town until recently, and she often lamented not being here when Auntie A died of late-stage ovarian cancer last January. I figured her kindness toward me stemmed directly from her devotion to my great aunt.

"It went okay," I said, allowing the thin brown dog to mosey over to her. Given his sluggish pace, he certainly wasn't going to jump up or grab her food bag. "He said he was sorry, so I guess that's a step in the right direction. He's never apologized before."

Vera quirked an eyebrow. "Well, now. Isn't that interesting. I wonder what brought that on."

I had to grin at her suspicious tone. "I don't think he had any motive, other than to tell me he's moving up in the world and he's broken things off with the...other woman. Well, women."

Vera's pale lips flattened. "Mm-hm."

Before I could race to Jake's defense—and why was I doing that anyway?—Charity walked over and looked at Vera. "Did you try the wrap?" she asked.

Vera shook her head, scratching behind the brown dog's ear. "I'm taking it with me, but I know it'll be delicious." She turned my way. "Charity's son Brian went to school with my daughter. She was the homeroom mom of the year, let me tell you."

Charity laughed. "All that work, and it didn't make a hill of beans of difference. Look at what happened to him."

Vera and I fell silent, knowing that Charity's son had gotten into drugs and run off with his second wife a few years ago, leaving his boy with Charity.

"I'm so glad you're going to be able to adopt Roman," I said quietly. "Is he in preschool now?"

Charity beamed, which made her pink cheeks look even rounder. "He is, and *law*, that boy is learning so fast! He told me his ABC's last night, all the way through."

"That's wonderful," Vera said.

Kylie's voice rang out in the Barks section, so I glanced over to see what was going on. She was talking loudly on the phone with someone. Thankfully, we didn't have any customers waiting.

Charity shook her head. "That sister of hers gives her fits," she said. "I've tried to get her to talk about it, since she's basically a surrogate mom to that girl. Their momma has issues, and their daddy, too. Kylie got out of their house as fast as she could."

Vera nodded. "Smart girl." She stretched out to pet the Pom mix, but the dog scurried off after a ball.

"I'd better get back over," Charity said. She smiled at Vera. "Let me know when you're visiting again, and I'll make you one of those toasted Caprese sandwiches I know you love."

Vera nodded. "And you tell me if you want to join the book club sometime," she said. Her hand lingered on the brown dog as Charity walked away.

"Are you interested in that one?" I asked hopefully.

She glanced down. "Oh no, hon, he's not really my speed. I was hoping for a more intimidating dog, you know, like a guard dog. I know you're just next door, but since I'm all alone in the house, I need a kind of alarm system. That way I'll have time to get my gun ready if someone breaks in."

I wasn't at all surprised that Vera owned a gun. She seemed exactly the kind of woman who'd know how to use it.

I smiled, envisioning Vera and me going target shooting with Bo someday. It wasn't outside the realm of possibility.

"Okay, I'll keep my eyes open for a dog like that," I said. "We get all kinds here."

Vera patted my hand. "I'm sure you do, dear. Now, I'd better get on home to eat my lunch. You and Bo have done a great job with this place." As she opened the gate to the dog section, she turned and said, "Keep your eyes open if that ex comes back around. He didn't seem very trustworthy."

That much I knew. Anyway, I doubted if Jake had stayed in town. He was probably hightailing it back to South Carolina, ready to take over the family business.

WHEN MY SHIFT finished and Bristol arrived, I slipped over to my place for a late lunch. After eating, I promptly dozed off on the couch. I started dreaming about Jake, so I was grateful when Coal sat on my feet and woke me up. He had made an unsuccessful attempt to squeeze in next to me.

I headed back to the cafe twenty minutes before I had to close up. After grabbing a white mocha latte from Jimmy, I sat down near the fireplace and watched the clientele milling around.

My attention sharpened when I realized that several customers were going out of their way to avoid Kylie, who was working a double shift. They seemed to be waiting until Jimmy returned to the register to place their orders. The morning news must have mentioned Kylie, or at least the fact that one of her weapons was discovered in Alec's back.

The formidable look on Kylie's face wasn't doing her any favors, either. She stood with her back to the world, resolutely churning out coffee drinks as if her life depended on it.

I was thinking about giving her a pep talk when she turned, glanced at an incoming customer, and dropped the soymilk container she was holding. I rushed over to help her wipe up the mess. "Are you okay?" I whispered.

As her eyes met mine, I saw something new in them—something that looked almost like fear. Shaking her head, she asked, "Would you mind if I headed out early? I can't seem to focus today."

I nodded. It certainly hadn't been an easy day for her, but her unease seemed directly linked to the man who'd just walked in. "No problem. Let me know how you're doing tomorrow."

Without even taking off her barista apron, Kylie was out the door like a shot. I finished mopping up, then stood to get a better look at the customer that seemed to have unsettled Kylie so badly.

He was a tall, burly man, roughly the same size as Jimmy. He had scraggly, combed-over black hair that was obviously a dye job. He'd already placed an order with Jimmy and was waiting at the other end of the counter to pick it up.

I worked up a friendly smile and walked over to him, determined to figure out who he was. "Hi, I'm Macy, and my brother and I own this cafe. I don't think we've seen you here before?"

The man extended his hand, so I reached out to shake it. After enveloping my hand in his own beefy, sweaty palm, he shook it, holding on a couple of moments too long.

"Doug Rucker," he said, shooting spittle onto the

countertop below. "Nice to meet you, Macy. Great little place you've got here."

"Thanks," I said, trying to keep my smile in place. "And what brings you here today?"

"I heard about your cafe through a friend. I thought I'd drop in and see what it's all about."

Jimmy came over and handed the man his coffee. I backed up a bit.

Doug's attention stayed focused on me. "I saw that girl Kylie leaving a minute ago. She works here, does she?"

I really didn't like his tone. My friendly façade was quickly melting. "And why would you be asking? Do you know her?"

He nodded. "I used to work with her dad, back in the day. Of course, she won't have nothing to do with him now. Too hoity-toity, I suppose."

Obviously, he didn't know Kylie very well. From what I'd heard, she had her own reasons to break things off with her parents. Our conversation was over.

"Thanks for stopping in," I managed. Turning away from the rude man, I headed into the back room to scrub off the rancid smell he'd left on my hands. It was no wonder Kylie didn't like Doug Rucker.

8

AFTER CLOSING, I stood on the cafe porch, trying to adjust the fall wreath on the door. Every time customers went in and out, its fake leaves fluttered to the ground. I was disappointed with it, since it hadn't been a cheap decoration.

As I was shoving leaves back into the twisted grapevine base, a deep voice behind me said, "Miss Hatfield?"

I turned. An older man with white-tipped blond hair stood a polite distance away, near the edge of the porch. From his expensive watch to his dress shirt, it was clear he was some kind of businessman.

"Yes, I'm Macy Hatfield," I said, curious as to what he wanted.

"I'm Nelson," he said, extending a hand. As I shook his, I couldn't help but notice his strong grip. Like Bo, this was a man used to taking charge. "I believe you have an employee named Kylie?"

Great. He'd probably seen Kylie's name mentioned in the news this morning, like the rest of my customers who'd been avoiding her all day. Maybe he was trying to get the inside scoop.

"And you are interested because...?" I asked.

"Oh, I'm sorry I didn't explain more. I want to help Kylie. I know she isn't close with her parents—I employed her father, you see, and I had to let him go due to his problems with gambling and drinking. I found out later that her mother was an even bigger alcoholic than him. Those girls don't have anyone looking after them." His eyebrows drew together. "Reading between the lines in the news, I got the feeling they're going to try to pin this murder on Kylie, even though I don't think she'd have it in her to do something like that. Do you?"

I gave a brief shake of my head. "I don't think so."

"Right. Well, I know her parents won't be able to help her with lawyer fees if it comes to that." He pulled a swank leather wallet from his back pocket and thumbed out a business card, which he passed to me. "If the police call her back in, would you mind giving me a call or text at that number, Miss Hatfield? I want to make sure she has a quality lawyer. We would need to keep it quiet, though, because I know she'd refuse help if I offered it directly. Please don't even tell her I was here."

He was right—Kylie wouldn't want to feel beholden to anyone. But I was pleased to see that she had a fairy godfather looking out for her.

I nodded. "I understand. I'll be happy to let you know if the police take her in again. I only wish I could afford to help her that way myself." Although I'd saved up a lot since opening the cafe, I was now making payments on my new SUV, so expensive lawyer fees seemed out of the question.

Nelson smiled, glancing into the front window. "What a

lovely cafe, not to mention a great concept, bringing shelter dogs in like that. All the best to you, Miss Hatfield."

Although he wasn't wearing a hat, I could imagine the sharp-looking man doffing a fedora toward me before turning to leave.

I shoved the last fallen leaves into the wreath and headed down the steps toward my place. Idly flipping the business card over in my hand, I stopped short, sucking in my breath.

Kylie's fairy godfather was none other than Nels Hartmann, the local paving magnate who regularly donated huge sums to charities. In fact, an entire wing at the hospital had been named for his widow, Edie.

The fact that Kylie's dad had torpedoed his own job with such a successful company was a tragedy. From what I'd heard, Hartmann Paving employees were well-paid and had good benefits. Auntie A had always warned us about the "devil grip" of alcohol, encouraging us to stay away from it. I gathered she'd had first-hand experience with alcoholism with her husband, Uncle Clive. He'd died in his early fifties, and I couldn't remember one time Auntie A had spoken fondly of him.

At least someone other than me had Kylie's back now. That meant I could concentrate a little more on getting things in place for the Barks & Beans anniversary celebration, something I knew Bo would want me to do.

As I closed my garden gate, a shiny black Jeep Wrangler parked along the opposite curb caught my eye. Jake had always wanted one of those. Peering closer, I caught a glimpse of sunlight bouncing off a head of blond hair. It *was* Jake sitting in the Jeep.

He seemed to be looking at the house across from me, but I knew it was an act. After all, there was no good reason for him to be sitting outside my cafe right around closing time unless he were waiting for me—or flat-out *watching* me.

My irritation growing, I opened the gate and marched straight over to the Jeep. Before I could rap on Jake's window, he got out and stood to his full height of six feet. This quiet power play failed to intimidate me, since my brother was an inch taller. Still, Jake gave the impression that he was bringing the full measure of his handsomeness to bear.

"Macy." He stooped to give me a quick hug before I could back out of it. I tried to ignore the feel of the muscles under his soft cotton shirt as he drew me into his chest—a place I had once felt safe. Gently releasing me, he said, "I thought I'd drop in and see if you would like to join me for a meal at the Greenbrier tonight."

He knew I loved the food at the top-notch resort. I fumbled for an excuse. "Don't you have to get back to the dealership?"

He shrugged. "Things are in transition mode right now, and I had some vacation time I wanted to use. I wanted to take in the West Virginia sights again."

I gave a snort of laughter. "Are you kidding me? Every time we came here for vacation, you griped about how you hated the mountains. You couldn't wait to get back to South Carolina, where 'at least they have Chipotle.' Don't you remember?"

His mesmerizing eyes met mine, and the ground seemed to shift under me. Why did he always have this effect on me? Why couldn't I fight it?

His tone low, he said, "You're right. I was a jerk. I said and did things I can't take back." He took a step closer, and the freshly shampooed smell of his hair wafted my way. "But Macy, am I such a bad guy? Didn't I treat you like a queen?"

Unfortunately, in most ways, he had. A series of tantalizing memories flitted through my head—the weekly bouquets of exotic flowers he'd brought me, the complimentary early morning texts he'd sent before going to work, and the many Saturdays he'd made me breakfast. Yes, he'd spoiled me, all right, which might explain why I hadn't seen through him earlier.

"Yes," I whispered. If only I could work up the willpower to walk away from him for good.

He gestured to my house. "So tell me the truth—you were planning on eating alone in there tonight, weren't you? Maybe some frozen dumplings or your favorite honey mustard chicken tenders?"

I wanted to punch him, he knew me so well. "Well—"

He tenderly placed one hand on my cheek, his fingers trailing down to my chin in a familiar gesture that never failed to stir me. "We didn't end things right. I want to make it up to you while I'm in town. Just one meal together, that's all I'm asking."

"Okay." Did I just say that?

He beamed. "Excellent. I'll plan to pick you up at seven." He jumped back into his Jeep, giving me a wave as he pulled out.

Crossing the road to my gate, I felt dazed. It was like something had taken over my body and made me say yes to Jake the Snake one more time. "You can walk out if things get bad," I muttered to myself. "You don't have to spend one extra minute with him."

When I unlocked the door, Coal bounded out to relieve himself in the yard. I leaned against the porch railing to wait for him. I really needed to work through my issues with Jake. Although I'd convinced myself that I'd gotten over him, some deep part of me had always understood that the moment he showed up in the flesh or said something to me in his smooth, knowing way, I'd be toast.

As Coal climbed the steps and pressed into my side, I patted the broad part of his back. I just needed to get through this meal with Jake, then I'd let him know I didn't want to hear from him ever again. After all, he'd cheated on me, so there was no way he could truly love me.

Right?

Coal cocked his head up at me, as if he knew my traitorous thoughts. "I'll break it off for good this time," I said.

But my words rang hollow, even to my own ears.

I FELT ashamed to spruce myself up for the date, but the Greenbrier wasn't just any restaurant. The posh resort had one-of-a-kind decor, boasting pinks and greens and patterns you'd never expect to see together. It was a unique and high-class experience to go there, so I wanted to try to look like I belonged.

By the time Jake picked me up, I'd managed to find a lacy navy blouse and a straight skirt that worked well with my nude heels. I added the artsy dangly earrings Summer had given me for Christmas—all the while thinking she'd *hate* to find out I was wearing them on a date with Jake—and checked my final appearance in my full-length mirror.

Thanks to plenty of time in the summer sun, I wasn't as pale as usual. My freckles had gotten noticeable on my arms and face. Although I'd made all kinds of resolutions to start jogging regularly with Bo—or at least to walk behind him—I hadn't succeeded at any of them, so my body was looking rather *zaftig*, as Jake used to call it. Back then, I asked him why he didn't just spit it out and call me plump, but he'd said the word zaftig better captured all my curvy enchantment. He'd let me know he loved my figure, which was something I really shouldn't be thinking about as I headed out on our date.

Stormy had settled into the quilt on my bed and was shooting me a green-eyed stare. She'd lost nearly all her little toys under various pieces of furniture, and I hadn't had time to fish them out, so she was probably bored. Coal tired easily after frolicking with her, and right now, he was looking longingly at his pillow.

"You miss Bo?" I asked, walking over to rub Stormy's ears.

She seemed to perk up as I said his name.

"I know, I miss him too." I sighed. What would Bo say if he knew where I was going tonight?

The doorbell rang. Coal took off down the stairs, barking furiously. I grabbed my purse and slipped into my shoes, then followed.

I told Coal to sit—which he refused to do—then I slowly opened the door. Jake stood off to the side, like he feared Coal would charge out and try to tackle him.

Given the way Coal was standing at attention and panting, I wouldn't put it past him. "Sit," I repeated, giving him a glare. But once again, my usually well-mannered dog ignored me. Without waiting to correct him, I slipped out the door, then locked it behind me.

"Sorry about that," I said, taking in Jake's attire for the evening. Sunglasses, camel-colored turtleneck that looked like cashmere, and fitted pants. He had an artlessly wealthy look, as if he were born to the gentry. Of course, he wore no wedding ring, and neither did I. I'd taken mine off the day he'd admitted to having affairs and said he was leaving me.

I needed to remember that day.

Jake's Jeep was surprisingly comfortable, allowing me to relax a little as we made small talk on our way to the Greenbrier. Once there, we headed straight toward the indoor steakhouse and placed our orders. Jake turned all his attention to me, which was an admittedly heady thing. He asked about my life after moving to West Virginia and seemed genuinely interested in my adventures.

"You grew up with Carolina—*the* Carolina from Carolina Crush?" he asked, marveling.

I was about to elaborate on our friendship when my phone buzzed in my purse. I grabbed it and looked at the screen, but didn't recognize the number. Yet something told me to pick it up, so I did.

"Hello," I said.

"Macy, it's me."

I pressed the phone closer. "Bo?" I asked. "Are you okay?"

"I'm just fine. I wanted to give you a call to catch up. Is this a good time?"

"Sure." I looked across the table at Jake, who was contentedly munching on a bite of his calamari appetizer. He raised his eyebrows at me, questioning. I mouthed the word, "Bo," then stood and walked to a sitting area just outside the restaurant.

"How's it going?" I asked.

"Good. I've found some great coffee beans here."

This was code for the fact that he was successfully gathering evidence against Leo Moreau. We'd worked out our undercover phrases ahead of time.

"That's great. How long will you be there?"

"I'm not sure. It could take awhile."

My heart sank. "What's that mean for the anniversary celebration? It's scheduled for this Saturday," I said.

"I know. I'm thinking you might have to handle it on your own." His voice was discouraged. "Is the planning coming along okay? And how's the cafe? Anything new there?"

Boy, was there ever. Our best barista was under investigation for murder, and the customers didn't even want to talk to her anymore. But these were the things I didn't want Bo worrying about while he was out of the country, working on a secret mission.

"Summer and I are figuring out the anniversary stuff, and yeah, everything's good at the cafe," I said.

There was a pause.

"You still there?" I asked, hoping we hadn't lost the connection.

"Sis, I know you, and I can hear you lying through the phone. What's going on at Barks & Beans?"

Since I knew I'd never shake him from this line of questioning, I resigned myself to telling him the whole truth. "We have a situation with Kylie. I'm not sure what to do about it."

I told him about Coal and me finding Alec's body in the antique car, about Kylie's sword stuck in his back, and about her sister's involvement with the dead man. After sharing that our customers were acting leery of Kylie, I asked, "What can I do to help? Kylie's determined to power through this, but I know she's hurting. She won't open up to me at all."

"You have to dial it back a little, Macy. Kylie's not a naturally friendly person like you are. She might not understand that you genuinely want to be there for her."

"I think she's been hurt a lot, maybe by her parents," I said.

"I'm sure she has." As usual, Bo's confident and comforting tone made me feel like everything was going to be okay. "Just keep reaching out to her—maybe in subtle ways—and eventually she'll realize she can trust you."

"I'll do that," I said, eager to try.

"How's Stormy?" he asked.

"She misses you. I do, too." I wasn't about to launch into the story of how she flooded my laundry room.

He sounded distracted. "Give her a hug for me. Okay, I have to run now. Listen, if things go sideways with Kylie, hire a good lawyer and I'll pay for it."

"Oh, but someone's already—"

"Gotta run," he said abruptly. "I'll be in touch again. Love you, sis."

"Love you too." The line went dead and I dropped my phone into my lap, staring at the brightly-colored couches around me. Bo was okay for now, but I hated that he didn't know when he'd be able to come home.

"You okay?" Jake hovered over me, his eyes concerned. "You just took off. They brought your salmon out already."

"I'm sorry," I said, knowing I shouldn't even apologize. "Bo's out of town, like I said, so I needed to touch base with him." I didn't mention how *far* out of town Bo was.

"Oh, sure. You coming back in?" he asked.

"Of course." I grabbed my purse and followed Jake back into the softly-lit restaurant, allowing myself to acknowledge that every minute I spent with him was a minute wasted. There were better guys in the world, more honest guys. I didn't have to do this.

But as I sat down at the table and he fixed me with that

knowing look and asked me how I was *actually* doing, tears sprang into my eyes. I felt very alone, and Jake could probably see that. I hated how weak I was around him, how easily his looks and words disarmed me.

Taking one lingering glance at his gorgeous face, I made a decision—a decision to protect myself. "I'm not doing so great, actually. I really can't be with you right now, Jake. Don't worry, I'll ask them to box up my food and I'll have my friend pick me up."

His fork, laden with a thick bite of steak, froze in midair. "Wait—what?"

Standing, I said, "Thanks for dinner. Maybe I'll text later, but please don't follow me." I darted over to the hostess desk and asked them to pack up my salmon and potatoes, then hurried out to call Summer.

Date night was over—and so was my lingering connection with Jake. I'd come to my senses, and I wasn't going to lose them again.

9

"Explain to me again why you went out with him," Summer demanded, pulling up to my curb.

"I really can't. It's a Jake thing," I said, grasping my paper bag and opening her car door. "Thanks again for picking me up at the drop of the hat like that. I promise I won't do that to you again."

"Riiight," she said. Her brown eyes got serious. "Listen, I don't mind at all—it's not like I was out on the town tonight. More like eating a popcorn supper surrounded by foster cats. But we both know your brother wouldn't like what you did."

"I know," I said. "I think talking to Bo was what woke me up a little. If he'd known where I was..."

Summer's lips twisted. "Oh, yeah. That wouldn't be good."

I stood. "Right, and that's why we can't tell him about Jake. Thanks again, girl. I'll see you in the morning."

Summer pulled away and I walked toward the house, half expecting to see Jake's Jeep parked in its regular spot.

My phone rang, so I balanced the food bag on the fence, then picked up.

Kylie's voice sounded high-pitched on the other end. "I need you to drop by my place," she said briskly.

"What do you mean? What's going on?"

"The police are here, and I need to go down to the station with them. I want someone to stay with Chelsea."

Wasn't Chelsea a big girl now? "Uh, sure, but why are they taking you in at this time of night?" I asked.

Voices sounded in the background as Kylie answered. "Because someone else just showed up dead—and this time, the body was in my front yard."

I DIDN'T EVEN BOTHER GOING into my house. Instead, I pulled the car keys out and jumped into my SUV, setting my food bag in the passenger seat. I really hoped the corpse in Kylie's front yard wasn't someone she knew.

As I pulled up to their place, lights were blazing and police officers were trampling the small patch of lawn out front. I didn't see a body, so they must've already removed it, but I did see Detective Hatcher standing just inside the front door, having an intense discussion with Kylie.

I moved their way and stopped on the edge of the porch, where I angled to the side and pretended not to listen.

"I *swear* today was the first time I'd seen him in five years." Kylie's voice teetered on the brink of hysterics. Although the sides of her dark hair were puffed out, the back was pressed flat to her head, like she'd been resting before things had hit the fan outside her door.

Detective Hatcher's voice was soothing, as if he knew he

was dealing with a live wire. "I won't keep you long at all," he said. "But given your history with the victim, we have to ask some more questions, and it'll be easier down at the station." He turned to me. "Macy, I'm glad you came by. Both Kylie and I will feel better knowing someone's with Chelsea right now."

"No problem," I said, shooting Kylie a questioning look. Who on earth showed up dead in her yard?

"I'll be right back—excuse me, ladies," the detective said, politely stepping around me into the yard to talk with an officer.

I rushed to Kylie's side. "What happened?" I demanded.

She motioned me indoors, where things were quieter. Chelsea was nowhere in sight.

"I went to take my trash can out for pickup, and I saw this...lump lying in my hedge. I looked closer and realized it was another dead body. It had been stabbed, just like Alec, only this time, it was with one of my long knives. I didn't touch it and called the cops."

"But the detective said you knew the dead guy?" I asked.

She gave a weary nod. "I didn't realize until they turned him over, but it was Doug Rucker, this man who—"

"He worked with your dad," I finished. "And he was the one at the cafe today when you left early."

"Yeah." Her eyes darkened. "Unfortunately, it didn't take long for the cops to discover that I knew Doug. And not in a good way." She shivered, pulling her sleeves down as if she were suddenly freezing, even though the house was warm. Her hazel eyes met mine for a moment before she dropped them and muttered, "When I was nineteen, he...assaulted me."

I couldn't stop myself from pulling her directly into a tight hug. "Oh, Kylie, honey, I'm so sorry."

Her stiffened body relaxed a moment in my arms, then she pulled back. "I'm okay." She glanced at the door, but the detective was still outside. "I didn't handle it well at the time. I did something stupid to get revenge on him. That's what's on the record."

"What do you mean—you keyed his car? Made prank calls?" Even as I asked, something told me Kylie wasn't the type to mess around with those petty kinds of retribution.

She didn't even blink. "I tried to light his house on fire, with him in it."

My mouth dropped open, but before I could think of something to say, the detective walked in.

"Okay, we can get going," he said. "Thanks again, Macy."

Kylie shot me a desperate look. "Chelsea's in her room. Please don't let her go anywhere tonight."

Still stunned over Kylie's fire-starting admission, I managed a somewhat reassuring nod. "Okay." In reality, I had zero confidence in my ability to keep the apathetic young woman at home.

The detective said, "I'll send her back as soon as I can."

Kylie's voice was frustrated. "But I have work tomorrow."

"I'll get someone to cover for you if we need to," I said. "Don't worry about things."

As Kylie walked out of the house, I took a deep breath. I'd never been comfortable with being the one in charge. While we were growing up, Bo was always the responsible protector who made sure I got places on time and did my homework. In the meantime, I threw all my efforts into flitting around the woods with my dogs like I didn't have a care in the world.

I guessed it was time for Chelsea and me to do a little growing up.

After striding over to the only bedroom door that was adorned with freaky posters, I gave it a sharp rap. "Chelsea, it's me, Macy Hatfield. Could you open up a minute?"

I stood in silence until the door finally swung open. Chelsea wore earbuds and her thumb hovered over her phone, as if I'd interrupted her texting. She focused on me, her eyes bored. "Yeah?"

I decided to get straight to the point. "I'll be staying with you here while Kylie's down at the police station. I'm going to sleep on the couch. Just let me know if you need anything, and for your own safety, stay in your room, okay?"

I tacked that last command on, hoping she wouldn't buck against it.

"Whatever," she said, swinging the door shut.

Really? A dead man had showed up in her front yard, her big sister had been taken in for questioning, and she was okay with "whatever?"

My Auntie A would've said Chelsea was "doless," which was a euphemism for lazy. I didn't think that was the case, though. Chelsea was rebelling against something—maybe her doless parents—and she was taking it out on her sister. Once again, I felt bad for Kylie, who was carrying the weight of the world on her shoulders right now.

And what on earth had happened when Kylie tried to light Doug Rucker's house on fire? Had she gotten caught in the process? Had the fire fizzled out? Had she managed to burn up part of the house before he escaped?

At least Doug had survived Kylie's arson attempt intact. Kylie said that her crime was on the record, so Doug would've been fully aware of who tried to torch his place—

and *why*. Kylie had been just over the age of a minor when he'd assaulted her, so I wondered if she'd even reported him. Given her parents' lack of concern, not to mention the fact that her dad had worked with Doug, it seemed pretty clear that Kylie had decided to bypass the traditional routes of justice and deal with Doug in her own way. Had she felt upset or relieved when she'd failed to burn his house down?

What absolute gall for Doug to show up in the cafe today, knowing that Kylie worked there. Had he wanted to taunt her with the fact that he was still alive and kicking? Intimidate her by bringing up painful memories? No wonder she'd acted fearful and left work as quickly as possible.

After getting a drink of water from Kylie's kitchen, I headed for the worn floral couch. Tugging a small fleece blanket over me, I tried to stop my thoughts from swirling. Chelsea's bedroom light continued to filter under her door, so I guessed she wasn't going to sleep anytime soon.

With a jolt, I realized that Summer was right. Kylie wasn't the kind of woman to be trifled with. In fact, she was capable of killing someone.

But surely she wouldn't have thought she could get away with using her own weapons to stab men she knew before dumping their bodies where they were sure to be found? It seemed extremely unlikely...unless she'd wanted to get caught, and I couldn't believe that. Kylie loved her job and she loved her sister. She'd never do anything to jeopardize her ability to provide a safe place for Chelsea to live.

No, something else was going on, but I couldn't understand what.

I attempted to stretch the tiny square blanket over my feet. Curling into a tighter ball, I wondered how Coal and Stormy were doing. I'd left plenty of food out, and Coal had been sleepy before I'd gone on the date, so he was probably conked out. I knew I didn't need to worry, because he had great bladder control for a dog that guzzled water all the time. I set my phone alarm so I could get over there early and let him out before I had to open the cafe. Hopefully Kylie would be home by then.

I was just drifting off to sleep when a very clear image of Jake flashed into my head. His gaze was soft, and his warm smile said that I was beautiful.

I rolled over, trying to erase the vision, but it was nearly impossible. I guessed we all had our own demons, only some of them were far prettier than others.

I SAT up in the darkness, glancing around. It took me a moment to place where I was, and a moment later, I realized why I'd woken up—someone was moving around in Kylie's living room.

"Who's there?" I demanded, jumping to my feet. I hadn't even thought to grab a kitchen knife in case Doug's killer returned.

"It's me, Kylie," she said. "Sorry for surprising you. I didn't realize you'd be on the couch. You could've slept on my bed."

I heaved a sigh of relief. "Oh, no. The couch is fine. I'm glad you're home." Grabbing my phone, I looked at the time. It was only two in the morning.

"They kept me awhile," she whispered. "We had to go over my records and things. You can go back to sleep. I'm going to grab a snack and get to bed."

As much as I wanted to ask Kylie about her history with Doug, I knew we both needed to sleep.

"Promise we'll talk more tomorrow," I pleaded, figuring Kylie would clam up in the cold light of day. "I want to help you any way I can."

Her quiet voice was thoughtful as she rummaged in the cabinet. "I promise," she said.

Lying back on the couch, I turned toward it and pulled the blanket snug. Detective Hatcher hadn't booked Kylie, so that was a good sign. Like me, he would've noted the convenient way the murder weapons—*Kylie's* weapons— were left in both dead bodies.

Hopefully, he had some other suspects lined up to investigate. Maybe tomorrow Kylie could give me a better idea of who might have it in for her, so we could keep an eye out at the cafe.

10

KYLIE WAS up before my alarm went off. When I struggled into a sitting position, she was bustling around the kitchen, already fully dressed and wearing makeup. She promptly offered me a latte, which I refused, even though I knew it would be amazing. I needed to get home and let Coal out.

I grabbed my purse and was just about to say goodbye when someone knocked at her door.

"I'll get it." Kylie walked over, so I backed up behind her.

Standing outside was an older man who was thin everywhere except in his noticeable paunch. His dark, graying hair was slicked back and his jeans were droopy. He leaned into the doorframe. "Glad to find you home. I knew I had to get up early to catch ye." He had a heavy Appalachian accent.

Since Kylie didn't recoil, I didn't step forward to intervene. She must know this guy.

She sighed. "Dad, what're you doing here? I've got to head out to work soon."

So this was Kylie's dad.

He gave me a long, measuring look. "And who's this?"

She rolled her eyes. "Well, it's none of your business, but it's my boss. Now what do you need?"

He took a moment to spit off the side of the porch, and I realized he had a chew of tobacco in his mouth. "I heard through Emmy that her Doug showed up dead last night in my daughter's yard. I told her I didn't know nothing about it." He peered in at her. "You never stopped hating him, did ye? Now tell me you didn't bump him off."

"Dad!" Kylie smacked a hand on the door. "Are you kidding me right now? No, I didn't kill Doug."

He gave her a shrewd look. "Well, I knowed you got called in afore when they found that Alec Marchand lying dead. Now there's one feller that deserved killin'. He looked good, but he was scum, peddlin' his drugs all around town."

Kylie glanced at me, and I gave her an encouraging half-smile. I needed to get going, but I didn't know if they had a back door. Besides, I was finding this conversation fascinating.

Her dad continued. "Speaking of that Alec, your momma and I want Chels to come back home, now she's not with him anymore. It's a real stroke of luck he's dead. Now there ain't no sense in her livin' with ye longer than need be."

The set of Kylie's jaw made it clear that no such transfer of residence was going to occur. "She'll be staying with me, Dad." She started to close the door. "I need to get moving."

He turned and spat again. "Suit yourself, but don't come cryin' if she gets with another lowlife." As he moseyed down the steps, he muttered, "And after all I've done for ye."

Kylie closed the door and turned. "Would you mind waiting just a minute, until he drives away? I don't want him cornering you out there."

"No problem," I said. "What did he mean saying 'after all I've done for you'? I thought you two had been on your own for awhile?"

"We have," she said, heading back toward the kitchen. "I honestly don't know what he meant. I've paid my own way since I was nineteen."

"It sounds like your dad and Doug were friends, then?" I asked.

She nodded. "That's what made things so difficult. I never told him what happened."

My heart went out to this tough-shelled, tattooed girl who'd been forced to face her trauma alone. "I'm here anytime you want to talk," I said. Throwing a glance at the microwave clock, I opened the door. "I'd better get going. Do you think Chelsea will be okay on her own?"

Kylie nodded. "I'll have the neighbor check in on her, and I'll be texting her throughout the day."

"Okay, I'll see you at work." I pulled the door shut behind me. As I stepped outside, the cheery skies and crisp fall air were at odds with the bloody splotch in the grass below. Logically, if Kylie didn't kill Doug, which I was convinced she wouldn't do—at least, not in such an undisguised manner —it had to be someone who was aware of her previous attempt on his life. Someone who'd used one of her weapons to make it look like she'd decided to go back and finish the job.

Maybe that was the key—looking into people who'd bought weapons from her. But I doubted Kylie kept any kind of record of the names of people she sold to, especially at huge events like the Ren Faire. I'd have to ask her if there was anyone she was close to who collected her weapons.

In the meantime, I dreaded what would happen once

Doug's death hit the news. Even if they didn't mention Kylie's knife, they'd surely state where the body was found, and anyone familiar with the area could put two and two together and discover it was Kylie's yard.

Life certainly wasn't getting any easier for Kylie. Clearly, someone wanted her out of circulation...but why?

From Tuesday until Friday, Summer and I focused on planning the Saturday celebration we'd been advertising for a couple of months. Kylie threw herself into developing the perfect specialty anniversary coffee drink, which she termed the "Double Dog Latte." The iced coffee started with a double shot of our best quality Costa Rican bean espresso. Caramel and white chocolate syrups were added to the base, and finally the delectable concoction was topped with whipped cream and white chocolate shavings. It was one of the best things I'd ever sipped on.

But Kylie wasn't the only one using her skills for the celebration. Every single one of our employees brought unique talents to the table. Milo amped up the social media ads and put up flyers at his parents' country club, as well as the upscale shops they frequented. Jimmy, our retired school bus driver, made sure all his friends in the school system heard about it. Bristol designed strings of decorative paws and bones and paired them with twinkle lights, which she strung around the cafe. Charity worked on perfecting her maple cream puff recipe, and she added a prosciutto croissant sandwich to the Saturday menu.

Summer assured me that she'd wash the dogs she'd chosen for the celebration with her best shampoo. She was bringing five total, which was the max number our Barks section could handle.

With all the bustle, I hadn't been able to catch up with Kylie about the murder investigations. I assumed that since she was working as usual, nothing new had come up—at least nothing pointing to her.

Friday night as I started closing, Kylie lingered behind, cleaning the coffee bar area one last time. Summer had already picked up the two shelter dogs we'd had that day, since she'd taken over that chore while Bo was out. I glanced around, once again awed by Bristol's ability to make the cafe look like a dog-lover's wonderland.

"I'm excited," I said, straightening the dog treats in the Barks section. "I've heard a lot of customers saying they plan to drop by tomorrow."

"Me, too." Kylie rustled around behind the counter.

There was a knock at the locked front door, and Kylie went over to open it. Her Ren Faire friend Joel walked in. He leaned down and gave Kylie a quick kiss on the cheek, and to my surprise, she actually smiled in return.

"Hi, Joel," I said, glad to see that Kylie seemed quite friendly toward him. "Fancy meeting you here."

He grinned and walked over. "I thought I'd drop by and catch up with Kylie." His eyes played over the Barks section. "Wow, this is some place you've got. I've never seen anything like it." One of his long blond curls tumbled onto his nose and he shoved it back. He and Kylie made a nice couple.

"I hope you'll be sticking around until tomorrow so you can join us for the anniversary celebration," I said. "Kylie came up with a fantastic new iced coffee for it."

"I do plan to come," he said. "Actually, I've decided to make a long weekend of it. I'm camping out in a tent over at

Moncove Lake." He jerked his thumb toward Kylie, who was busy behind the bar again. Lowering his voice, he said, "I'm hoping she'll feed me some while I'm in."

"I heard that. Of course I'll feed you." She came around and tucked an arm under Joel's. "You've told me many times that your cooking skills only extend to making ramen noodles."

"So, are you two an item again?" My cheeks colored as the question popped from my mouth, which seemed to have been taken over by the spirit of Auntie A.

Joel's eyebrows raised, but Kylie's face stayed composed. "We're playing things by ear."

I recalled what Joel had said about how their initial breakup occurred—that Chelsea had told her sister that Joel had gotten fresh with her. Given the way Joel couldn't take his eyes off Kylie, not to mention Chelsea's overall impertinence, Kylie should've immediately deduced that Chelsea was lying. Instead, for some strange reason, she'd chosen to believe her sister and had broken up with Joel.

"Speaking of food, we'd better get going," Kylie said. "I want to get the burgers on the grill. I'll see you tomorrow, Miss Hatfield."

"See you then." As Joel and Kylie walked out the door arm in arm, I felt a sharp, stupid pang of loneliness. Jake and I used to walk that way. For a split second, I thought about texting him to ask if he'd gotten home okay. I'd never followed up after my abrupt exit from the restaurant on Monday night. And with all my planning for the celebration, I'd managed to shove any thoughts of Jake aside.

Telling myself I didn't owe Jake an apology, I hit the lights and headed through the connecting door to my place. Coal was waiting on the other side, tail wagging. Was there anything more welcoming than a dog? Stormy certainly wasn't sitting there, her every attention fixed on my return, but then again, she wasn't my cat. Maybe she did that for Bo.

I petted Coal for a moment, then headed down the hallway, holding my breath that Stormy hadn't wormed her way into another off-limits locale. Thankfully, I found her sitting on the couch, deeply engrossed in licking herself down. As I watched her dainty cleaning job, I had to admit that she did have her cuter moments.

I let Coal out the back, taking a moment to breathe in the fresh air, which was laced with the earthy scent of impending rain. While I had hopes that tomorrow would be a pretty day, a little rain wouldn't make much difference since we were holding our celebration indoors. I did feel bad for Joel, though, since he would be sleeping out in the elements the next couple of nights. Hopefully his tent was newer and watertight.

I sat down as Coal sniffed at a hole in the fence, and my thoughts drifted to Kylie. It would definitely do her good to have someone like Joel to talk to. Goodness knew she hardly opened up to anyone else, and with a life story like hers, which included alcoholic parents, trauma, and a criminal past, she needed the support.

It was sweet to see how often Joel was traveling up to West Virginia. He seemed truly devoted to Kylie. I wondered if the fatal flea market was the first time they'd seen each other since their Ren Faire summers.

As Coal attempted to poke his large nose into the hole, something occurred to me. If Kylie hadn't been a suspect in two murder investigations, she might not have started getting so close to Joel. Her rare vulnerability had made her more open to his romantic intentions.

My eyes narrowed as my thoughts took a very dark turn. Yes, things had worked out in Joel's favor, all right. Surely he wouldn't have been so desperate for her love that he could have actually planned a couple of murders to get her attention.

No, that was the kind of psycho stuff you saw in movies. I doubted it happened much in real life. I stood, whistling for Coal to come in.

As my thoughts flew to Jake yet again, I cringed at his inexplicable, ceaseless power over me—kind of like Edward from *Twilight*. Firsthand experience had taught me that love could be a cruel taskmaster. Maybe there was something in my rather random suspicion of Joel...maybe he had an obsessive streak I'd subconsciously picked up on. I decided to keep an eye on him tomorrow, just in case.

11

SATURDAY MORNING WAS a whirl of activity, with all our employees helping in the cafe. Charity and Milo set up the foods in the glass display cabinet, Kylie and Jimmy prepped the coffee bar for the influx of drink requests with our buy-one-get-one deal, and Bristol and I made sure the Barks section was in spit-spot condition. The five dogs Summer had dropped off were beautiful. I knew she'd chosen the cream of the crop for today. From the friendly red-haired Irish setter mix to the tiny terrier blend, each dog seemed to have a winning personality, not to mention a beautifully cleaned and brushed coat. I felt pretty confident every one of them would get adopted.

Bristol took photos as the customers started to pour in. I watched closely to see if they avoided Kylie, since Doug's death had hit the news, but it seemed they were more interested in taking advantage of our deals than worrying about whether a murderer was brewing their coffee. Besides, the news had only mentioned the neighborhood where

Doug's body was found, and not Kylie's address, so people likely hadn't made the connection.

From time to time I glanced over to the coffee bar, half convincing myself that Bo would walk out any minute to brew up some drinks. After all, he was the one who'd masterminded this entire business, from start to finish. He was the one who'd chucked a good deal of his money into developing a cafe where I could use my dog-loving abilities for the greater good. In creating the Barks & Beans Cafe, he'd given me a safe place to land when infidelity and divorce had torn my world apart. I owed him so much.

Bristol nudged me. "Look at that dude—isn't he some kind of famous actor?"

I followed her gaze and could've dropped through the floor. Jake Hollings had not left town yet. Jake Hollings was, in fact, throwing a brilliant smile my way as he headed for the coffee bar.

"He's an actor, all right, but not the famous kind," I said. "He's actually my lying ex-husband."

Bristol's grin faded. "Oh, Miss Hatfield, I'm sorry. What's he doing here?"

"Hanged if I know," I said, adopting a choice phrase I'd pulled from Agatha Christie books and utilized often during my teen years.

Doubtless picking up on the waves of irritation rolling off me, Bristol dashed over to deal with the setter mix. He was sniffing at a roaming toddler so vigorously he might actually knock him over.

Refusing to cower in my own cafe, I stood and stalked over to Jake, who was now third in line. "I didn't realize you were sticking around so long," I said. "You must have had quite the vacation time saved up. You've been here, what, a week now?"

He nodded, but his perfectly styled blond bangs didn't budge. "I wanted to drop in and celebrate with you. I know Bo's out of town."

As if *Jake* could ever be a stand-in for my loyal and loving brother.

It was Jake's turn to order. As he stepped up to the counter, Kylie asked, "What'll it be, sir?" Her concerned eyes darted my way. She wasn't sure who this guy was to me.

I might as well enlighten her. I mean, why not bring *all* my employees in on this train wreck? "Kylie, this is my ex-husband, Jake. Jake, this is Kylie. She makes an amazing foam-art latte."

He grinned in his winsome way. "That sounds delicious. I'll have a large caramel latte, then." He peered into the glass cabinet. "And maybe one of those croissant sandwiches. Thanks."

I forced a smile. "Well, I'd better get back over to the dogs. Have a good visit."

He took hold of my elbow in a smooth, gentle motion. "Would you mind staying with me a sec?"

Reluctantly, I waited as he paid for his order and took his sandwich. He led me over to the pick-up end of the coffee bar, where he turned and ran a caressing hand down my arm. "Do you think you could take your lunch break early and join me?"

My face must've given him an answer, because he reddened slightly and dropped his hand. "I'm sorry, I shouldn't have asked. I can see how busy things are for you. Maybe I'll text you sometime later, like tonight."

I didn't want him to text tonight. And I didn't even want

to *think* about how many days he was planning to stay in Lewisburg. Why was he sticking around, anyway? Didn't he have important business to get back to? Had he gotten fired and felt too ashamed to tell me? Or was he seriously trying to rebuild some kind of loving relationship between us?

"Sure, whatever," I mumbled. After whirling around, I skulked back to the Barks section, where Bristol was waiting for me, her dark eyes wide. I was embarrassed that all my employees had to witness the inappropriate and downright fawning behavior of my ex. "He just wanted to talk," I explained.

She gave an understanding nod. "He seems pretty hung up on you...and I'm guessing he's the kind of guy who's hard to say no to," she said.

"You're wise beyond your twenty-three years," I said. "Yes, he's a hard one to refuse, but I'm determined to keep doing it. I can't afford to let Jake Hollings get under my skin again."

As one of the dogs pranced in front of us, Bristol gave me a low high five. "More power to you," she said.

Power was something I'd never felt in my relationship with Jake, but I needed to step up and take it back. He had to understand that my life no longer revolved around him—no matter how hard he was to say no to.

JAKE WAS LONG GONE by the time I took a lunch break. As I bit into one of Charity's ham and cheddar sandwiches, I tried to let my tension go and focus on the good. The anniversary celebration was turning out to be an unparalleled success. I'd had three people ask about adopting shelter dogs, and Jimmy reported that sales were through the roof. Bo would be so pleased.

Joel dropped in, looking somewhat the worse for wear. Although today was clear and a bit chilly, last night there had been a few thunderstorms. I doubted he'd been able to sleep soundly in his tent.

After taking a few minutes to place an order with Kylie, he plopped into a chair by the fireplace. Bristol and I watched him from our seated positions on the dog mat. About five minutes later, Kylie took off her apron, grabbed a sandwich, and joined him.

"I think she's into him," Bristol observed. "Although it's a little hard to tell."

"I think so, too," I said. A small dog trotted over and rested her nose on my lap, so I stroked her black head. She hadn't gotten any interest yet, so I'd have to talk her friendliness up to incoming customers.

"He seems nice enough," Bristol added.

I was about to reply when a woman walked into the cafe, glanced around, then made an obvious beeline for Kylie's table. She was probably in her early fifties and sported a tan rain jacket, thick-soled tennis shoes, and a well-worn purse. Her faded hair was pulled back into a loose bun.

I sensed she had some kind of business with Kylie. Hoping she wasn't a town busybody come to point out Kylie's involvement with the murders, I crept closer to the low brick divider wall so I could listen to what she said. Bristol politely gave me space and busied herself with the dogs.

Kylie's voice held a note of uncertainty as she greeted the woman. "Emmy," she said, jumping to her feet and pulling a chair over to their table. "Please, have a seat."

Emmy hooked her purse over the chair back, then slowly sat down.

"How are you?" Kylie asked. "I'm sorry about—"

The woman's harsh voice contrasted with her soft appearance. "I know you're not sorry."

I held my breath, but the woman continued, her eyes softening. "Well, not any more than I am. He was a terrible man, and didn't you know it, Kylie Baer. I never doubted your story, that he'd done to you what he'd done to other girls along the way. Many's the time I wished I could've done him in myself, if you want to know the honest truth."

I had to assume that this woman was Mrs. Doug Rucker. And it would seem that Mrs. Rucker was not in any way, shape, or form a grieving widow.

Joel, who looked uncomfortable with the direction of the women's conversation, angled to face the fire. He was right to assume that Kylie wouldn't want others listening in on this, but as her boss, I needed to make sure someone menacing hadn't walked into our cafe. Thankfully, Mrs. Rucker didn't seem to be attracting any attention to herself.

The older woman extended a hand, cautiously patting Kylie's tattooed one. "All those years ago, I knew you'd waited until I was out of the house before you burned it." Tears sprang into her eyes. "When I came home to all the fire trucks, I hoped the blaze had eaten him alive in his bed. But we had no such luck, did we?"

Kylie swiped at the corner of her eyes. "No, ma'am."

Emmy Rucker sniffed. "I came over to tell you that I'm proud of you. I'm proud that you stood up to that brute, something I was never able to do." She pointed to herself. "Look at me. I'm just a shell of the woman I once was."

Kylie shook her head. "No, ma'am, you aren't. I hope you

can get back to teaching. I know a lot of kids who loved your classes."

"Thank you, but I'm not sure I have the stamina for it anymore." Mrs. Rucker offered a weak smile. "Your parents never did understand what a gem you were, did they? You always had your head screwed on straight, Kylie. Your mom told me you were working here, so I just wanted to come over and...I don't know what exactly." She gave a brief, hysterical giggle. "Celebrate, maybe?"

Kylie dropped her gaze to the table, so I couldn't tell what she was thinking. Sure, celebrating a man's death seemed a little extreme, but Doug Rucker had been the worst kind of human being. The kind who got away scot-free after hurting women. Come to think of it, Alec Marchand had been the same kind of man—someone who used others to get what he wanted and never considered the consequences.

Emmy gathered her purse from the chair and pulled the strap over her shoulder. She gave Kylie a deferential nod as she stood. "I'm sure we'll stay in touch. You take care, young lady." She strode out the door, her head higher than it had been when she entered, as if buoyed by her interaction with Kylie.

Kylie turned to Joel and murmured something to him. I drew back into the Barks section, thankful that Doug Rucker's widow hadn't come bearing any ill-will toward Kylie. If anything, it was just the opposite.

I wondered how closely the police were investigating Emmy. After all, she'd just admitted that she'd wanted her husband dead for a long time. Had she finally taken matters into her own hands and stabbed him to death?

But that didn't add up, because Doug's body was discovered smack in Kylie's lawn, killed by one of her knives.

Given Emmy's words of praise today, I couldn't believe she would have tried to pin it on Kylie...unless she was playing some kind of mind game with her.

I peeked out at Kylie again. She was brushing crumbs from the table as Joel stood. He gave her a halfhearted smile and walked out. She didn't even look up.

What had he said to her?

Or had Kylie scared him away by confirming what Emmy was insinuating—that she'd been the one to bump Doug off?

I needed to have a long chat with my best barista soon.

12

Dylan texted that he was sorry he couldn't drop in for the anniversary celebration, but he had a big showing for his D.C. artist today. He'd advertised it at the Greenbrier Resort and so far, he'd had a good turnout. I texted back that things were going well at Barks & Beans and that I hoped he'd sell a lot of pieces.

Vera dropped by around four, after Bristol, Milo, and Jimmy had already gone home. Business typically dropped off at this hour. Although we had a loyal after-work crowd, most people went elsewhere for dinner.

Vera looked like she'd just gotten her short gray hair trimmed, and she was wearing silver hoop earrings, which was an unusual touch for her. She came straight over to the Barks section, leaning over the divider to greet me.

"Were you out on the town today?" I asked.

She surprised me by saying, "I was out on a date, actually. At my age, you go on dates during the daytime hours." She winked.

I was dying to ask who she was seeing, but that would be

the height of rudeness. Besides, I didn't know many people in the over-sixty set.

As if sensing my curiosity, Vera continued. "I don't think you know him, since he's not really the type to get out and about much. It's Randall Mathena. He's retired from the railroad."

I shook my head. "No, I haven't met him yet, but be sure to tell him about the cafe. Maybe he'll drop in for coffee sometime."

"I sure will, hon. Actually, I came by to see if you have any new dogs in today. I'm ready to make a good canine friend." She peered into the Barks section.

Glancing around, I realized that all the dogs had been spoken for except the little terrier mix. I walked it over toward Vera. "This is the only one that hasn't been adopted today, but I know you wanted a bigger dog, right?"

Vera's face fell, despite the irresistibly hopeful gaze the little dog bestowed on her. "That one looks adorable, but yes —I need something bigger. More guard dog. It doesn't have to be as big as Coal, of course. Just big enough to make an intruder think twice." She sighed. "Maybe I'll grab a tea while I'm here and say hello to Charity."

Her old friend waved her over, so Vera headed toward the coffee bar. I'd have to ask Summer to flag any medium to large dogs that got checked into the shelter, so we could give Vera first dibs.

Someone flung open the cafe door. I glanced over and did a double-take when I saw what was heading straight for me. A curly-haired golden Labradoodle pulled at its leash, tugging Summer directly toward the Barks section, as if it were homing in on it.

I'd know that flighty dog anywhere, from the wild look in

her small eyes to her rounded mouth, which always looked like it was smiling. I couldn't help myself. Jumping to my feet, I held out my hands and shouted, "Waffles!"

Summer was already apologizing as she neared me. "I'm *so* sorry." She wrapped the leash tighter and opened the doggie gate to bring Waffles in. "Oh my word, I would never bring her in here unless I had to."

"I don't mind," I said. "You know I think she's sweet. It's Bo who doesn't want her in the cafe."

"Yeah, she's sweet but dumb," Summer lamented. "As you might have guessed, her latest adoptive family had some issues with her. She's back to stealing food from kids' plates, and now we can add terrorizing the aging family cat to the list of her skills, as well."

As she unleashed Waffles, the dog sat right down next to my feet and lifted a paw for me to shake. I grinned. "But Summer, just *look* at how well-behaved she is. How can you be so hard on her?"

Summer sighed. "I know, right? If only she'd keep that up. But we both know that's just a smokescreen." She dropped to her knees, her long patchwork skirt flowing around her as she scratched behind Waffles' ears. "I do believe there's the perfect home for her...somewhere. I just can't for the life of me seem to match her up with the right people."

"How many homes has she gone through now?" I asked.

"I've lost count," Summer said. "Anyway, they're cleaning a kennel for her at the shelter as we speak." She patted the dog's curly head. "I guess it's a big welcome home for you, Waffles."

The dog gave a sad whine and turned her little eyes toward me.

I shook my head. "Aw, as much as I like you, girl, Coal's plenty enough dog for me. Besides, I don't think you two would get along."

Summer nodded. "Yeah, I agree. Coal isn't the kind of dog that would appreciate fighting for attention—and Waffles demands *all* your attention, for sure."

I tossed a ball, and Waffles tore off after it. She was just returning the slobbery toy to me when Vera stepped over to the divider.

"Did I see you bring a new dog in here?" she asked hopefully.

Summer shot me a desperate look, shaking her head in warning.

"Uh, yes, but this dog is kind of a unique case," I hedged.

Vera's eyes brightened as she watched Waffles play. "What a gorgeous dog! I just want to pet her beautiful fur. It reminds me of my daughter's curly hair. Would you mind?"

Before I could caution her, Vera placed her cup of tea on a table and opened the dog gate. I fumbled to grab Waffles' collar, but didn't manage to snag it in time. As Vera stepped in, Waffles charged right for her.

"No!" I lunged toward her, but she was already out of reach.

Summer rushed over, ready to tackle the dog, but just before Waffles reached Vera, she stopped short and dropped into a sitting position at the older woman's feet. The only thing moving was her tail, which steadily flipped back and forth on the doggie mat.

I gave a nervous laugh. "She's a total wild card," I said. "We never know what she's going to do next."

Vera stroked Waffles' soft ears, her look one of

wonderment. "What a beautiful girl," she crooned, as if the two of them were in a world of their own.

Summer and I exchanged equally horrified glances. What kind of person would dare to pawn this unruly dog off on such a kind neighbor? I couldn't bring myself to do it, no matter how badly Waffles needed a home.

But as I watched dog and human interact, I realized I wasn't going to have to pawn Waffles off at all. She was selling herself, without any help. Her behavior for Vera was stellar, as if she'd just been introduced to her bestie for life.

Summer leaned in and whispered, "I have to say, I've never seen Waffles respond this way to anyone."

"I agree," I whispered back. "But now what?"

Summer shrugged. "We can warn her of the risks...give her the history."

Vera seemed to come out of her doggie-trance. "What risks do you mean?"

Apparently, we hadn't been whispering so quietly. I stared at Summer, silently willing her to share the rather preposterous background story on Waffles.

Summer introduced herself as the shelter owner. After taking a deep breath, she launched into Waffles' tale, sparing no detail. Vera took a seat and listened, her eyes occasionally shifting from Summer down to Waffles, who was now lying belly-up at her feet.

As Summer concluded her woeful recount, Vera gave a long look at Waffles, who'd taken to rolling around on her back. I held my breath, waiting for my neighbor's verdict. Although a large part of me wanted to see Waffles have another chance at a good home, the rest of me questioned whether petite little Vera could handle some of Waffles' crazier antics.

But when Vera gave a slow determined nod, I knew things had been decided. "I want Waffles," Vera said firmly, her brown eyes meeting mine. "Yes, she's got a lot of energy, but we can run that off in my big fenced yard. She chases cats and chickens, but I don't have any. And I'll work with her on her indoor bathroom accidents and food-snatching habits."

"Are you sure?" I blurted out, desperate to keep my friend from biting off more than she could chew. "It might make your book clubs difficult."

She waved a dismissive hand. "That's what dog crates are for. She'll have a safe, cozy place to hang out when I'm not around." She patted Waffles' pale stomach. "She's fixed, I assume?"

"Oh, definitely," Summer said.

"Good. I'd like to get her as soon as I can. I'll need to grab some supplies, but would I be able to drop by your shelter tonight and pick her up?" she asked.

I must not have grasped the full extent of Vera's loneliness, given her burning desire to bring Waffles home.

Summer smiled, and I knew she'd softened to the idea. "Of course."

Vera gave Waffles another affectionate pat before grabbing her tea and heading out. Summer turned to me, her look disbelieving. "I'd never in a million years have seen that one coming."

A grateful smile spread across my face. "Me neither, but I have a feeling that for the first time in her life, Waffles has actually bonded with someone."

"And she'll want to please her," Summer added.

"Let's hope."

Summer pulled her hair back and snapped an elastic

over it, unwittingly giving herself a stylish ponytail. "I'll take these guys back and get them ready for their new homes," she said, giving me a pat on the back. "And by the way— great job with placing dogs today, Macy. Things were hopping at the shelter with all that paperwork. I can't believe five dogs were adopted thanks to one event—that has to be a record."

"Bo will be thrilled," I said.

We both had a moment of silence for Bo, who was busy doing who knows what. The dogs started getting antsy, which snapped Summer back to attention. "Okay. I'd better get rolling. Thanks again, my friend."

"Anytime."

After Summer left and Charity waved goodbye, I tidied the dog section before heading over to see how Kylie was faring. I was curious as to what had happened to make Joel leave so abruptly, but I doubted Kylie would open up about it. Still, I wanted to make myself available in case she had any desire to talk.

"You doing okay?" I asked.

Kylie turned away from the espresso machine and looked at me. I couldn't identify the emotions swirling in the depths of her hazel eyes. She seemed to take a moment to consider, then finally spoke.

"The customers were okay with me today, so that's going better," she said.

I hadn't even broached the topic of their reluctance to talk to her after Alec Marchand's death hit the news, so I was glad she'd brought it up. "I'm sorry they were like that. It's just a small town and all..."

"I know," she said. "Sometimes I hate it, but most of the time it's comforting. That's why I stuck around when I moved out. I can't explain it, but I like living near the mountains."

I couldn't believe it. Kylie and I had something in common, after all. I could talk for hours about the Appalachians and what they brought to my life. But this wasn't the time. Kylie had shared information without my prodding, which I took as an indication that friendship wasn't out of the question.

I couldn't blow it, so I chose my next words carefully. "I'm glad Joel made it here today. Oh, and I saw that lady who came in and talked with you."

Kylie dropped the cleaning rag on the counter and leaned toward me. "You know, I honestly hadn't seen Emmy Rucker in years—she's Doug Rucker's wife. It was like once she quit her teaching job five years ago, he kept her locked at home or something."

"But wasn't he friends with your dad?"

She sighed. "Yeah, but only because they worked together in the same paving company. Dad got fired for drinking on the job, though. Doug was probably still working in paving when he died, I guess."

"Was your mom friends with Emmy at all?"

Kylie shook her head. "Not really. Emmy was more...let's say *upstanding* than my mom." She didn't elaborate.

I decided to return to the topic of Joel, since Kylie was actually conversing with me. Trying to sound casual, I asked, "How's Joel doing in his tent? I thought of him out there when it stormed last night."

She shrugged, and I could almost feel her pulling back into herself. "He said he was okay. He only had one leak, so he used his pot to catch the water."

I attempted one more question. "Is he sticking around tomorrow, then?"

She sprayed the rag and turned to wipe the back counter. "I don't think so. He'll head out early tonight. He asked me to be his girlfriend again, and I, uh...it just wasn't a good time."

I figured she needed a hug, but I knew she wouldn't accept one. "I'm really sorry. It seemed like you two have a good connection."

She turned around. "I know. And he's willing to stick by me, even knowing my weapons were found in dead bodies. But I can't commit to anything in the middle of all this, you know? Not until the police clear my name."

She said that like she actually believed they would. I sincerely hoped that would be the case, but it didn't seem like they were busy hunting down other leads. At least I knew we had the fallback option of a high-priced lawyer if Kylie got taken into custody, thanks to Nels Hartmann.

"I can't understand what you're going through right now, but just know that I'm here for you, okay?" I grabbed my keyring from my pocket. "You about ready to head out?"

"Yeah. Hang on a sec." She put the cleaning supplies away in the back room, then returned. As we stepped out onto the front porch together, she gave me a slow smile. "I know you're there for me, Miss Hatfield. I've never doubted that. You're a loyal kind of person, and I really appreciate it."

I felt like I'd received one of Kylie's highest compliments. In the moment, I wanted to ask her to call me "Macy" instead of "Miss Hatfield," but I decided it wouldn't be fair to our other employees to set a double standard like that.

We split up on the curb, where she headed for her car and I walked toward my place. There were no black Jeeps in sight, so I breathed a sigh of relief.

After letting Coal out, I joined him in my flower garden, trying to envision where I might squeeze in a bagful of large tulip bulbs. Jimmy's wife Jenny was an avid gardener, and when she'd split up her show-stopping ruffled violet tulips, she'd sent some over for me.

Near the garden gate, my eyes were drawn to a dried up patch of boring yellow daffodils. Making a snap decision, I headed for my garden shed to grab gloves and a trowel. The daffodils could be moved along the far border of the garden. Jenny's tulips would make a much better conversation piece by the entry gate.

I'd just sunk the trowel into the dirt when my phone buzzed. Coal loped over, his considerate look conveying the message that he'd be happy to help me out by answering the phone.

"Thanks. I just wish you could, boy." I peeled off a glove and pulled the phone from my back pocket. I was surprised to see it was Kylie. Maybe she was in the mood for more chitchat?

"I need to call in a favor," she said. "Could Chelsea and I come over for a little while and hang out with you?"

Wondering what would place Kylie in such dire straits that she had to ask me, I readily agreed. "Sure. I was just thinking of ordering takeout. But what's going on?" I asked.

"Detective Hatcher is here with some of his men, and I agreed to let them search my house."

13

"You DID *WHAT*?" I practically yelled into the phone.

Kylie's voice was calm. "I said they could search the place," she repeated. "I don't have anything to hide. Anyway, it sounded like if I said no, he'd eventually get a warrant. I figured if I complied quickly, that would look best."

Apparently, Kylie hadn't considered that her sister had recently been dating a drug dealer...which meant she could be hiding all kinds of things in that cloistered bedroom of hers.

"Are you sure about this? What did Chelsea say?" I asked.

"I didn't ask her. She's coming back from work in about five minutes, so when she gets here, we'll come over."

I could only imagine the kind of blowup that was about to go down at the Baer household, but I didn't want to borrow trouble. Hopefully, Chelsea was just as clean as Kylie assumed she was.

"Okay, no problem. Just come on up to the door and knock," I said. "You know how Coal is with the doorbell."

"I'm looking forward to seeing him again," Kylie said.

As we said goodbye, I peeled off my other glove and scratched Coal's head. His heavy tail thumped into my ankle. "Well, it looks like we'll be having company soon." I grabbed the trowel. "Let's head in and make sure your feline friend hasn't destroyed the place, shall we?"

As I returned things to the garden shed, I hoped Kylie's house would be the only thing to get flipped upside down today...and not her entire life.

KYLIE AND CHELSEA showed up half an hour later, just after the Chinese food had been delivered. Although Chelsea looked like her typical sullen self, she didn't show any signs of concern about the police search. This came as a relief to me, since that probably meant she didn't have any of her dead boyfriend's drugs to hide. She hadn't struck me as an addict, but I knew that opioid addiction was often hard to recognize.

Coal was thrilled to see Kylie again, although he was a bit more hesitant around Chelsea. He kept bumping against Kylie's legs and staring up at her.

"He really likes you," I said, setting the Chinese containers on the table.

"He's the kind of dog I'd choose if we could have a dog in our rental," Kylie said. "I'm hoping to buy the house someday, but I haven't saved up enough yet."

Chelsea took a large helping of pepper steak out and dumped it onto her lo mein. "Our place is so tiny, the police will probably have it searched in under twenty minutes."

Her disrespect was nearly palpable. I waited to see if

Kylie would scold her, but then again, as Charity had pointed out, she was her sister, not her mother. I was as easygoing as the next girl, but I hated to see Chelsea turning up her nose at the house Kylie had worked hard to provide. "Well, I think it's the perfect size," I said. "It's cozy."

Chelsea slurped up a noodle. "At least until you live there."

Kylie frowned. "Chels." She took a bite of sesame chicken.

"What are the police even looking for?" I asked. "Did they have some kind of reason to search your place?"

Kylie nodded, taking a sip of sweet tea. "Oh, yeah. Detective Hatcher said he finally got the full autopsy report on Alec Marchand, and it wasn't what they'd expected in the preliminary findings. The sword had definitely killed him, but he was rendered unconscious by a date-rape type of drug first."

Well, this certainly threw a new spin on things. "So they're searching your house for that drug?"

She grabbed an egg roll. "I guess so. I'd never even heard of it—GBH or something."

"GHB," Chelsea corrected.

Kylie and I both turned to stare at her. "How did you know that?" Kylie asked.

Chelsea shrugged. "Alec mentioned it a couple of times. I just remember because he said its street name is 'Georgia home boy.'"

Kylie's look darkened. "So you were dating a guy who was familiar with date-rape drugs? Didn't that strike you as vaguely repulsive?"

Chelsea simply laughed, which made me recoil. A young girl like her shouldn't be laughing off something as serious as dating a predator. Alec truly seemed to have been a regular 'lowlife,' as Kylie's dad had aptly put it.

Coal, who was sitting on his pillow, cocked his head at me. I knew he was probably clued into my feelings toward Chelsea. Stormy was nowhere to be seen, and hadn't been since Kylie and Chelsea walked in. It was odd for the bold cat to shy away like that...

I jumped up, dropping my napkin to the table. "Excuse me a sec. I need to check something."

I speed-walked toward the laundry room, but the door was still closed. Coal raced up behind me, anxious to help. "Where's Stormy?" I asked.

He looked around, then headed toward the stairs. I followed him up to my room, but there was no sign of the Calico. Dropping to my knees, I checked under the bed, but she wasn't under it. Finally, I looked in my closet and a sad meow sounded above me. My eyes widened in disbelief.

Stormy had somehow squeezed her body into a round-bottomed glass vase I'd set on my shelf. Her head was squished into the neck of the thing, her green eyes wild where they pressed against the glass.

"Oh, you have *got* to be kidding me!" I yelled. Coal gave a nervous yip, anxious for me to rescue his little buddy. "How on earth am I going to get you out of there, you crazy cat?" I carefully reached up and took the vase from the shelf, Stormy yowling all the while.

After looking at the vase from different angles, I concluded that if Stormy couldn't extract herself, I was going to have to take the drastic measure of breaking the glass at the bottom to let her out.

"You okay up there?" Kylie shouted from downstairs.

"Uh, yeah. I just have to deal with something real quick."

I headed into my bathroom and glanced around for a tool that might break the vase with as little shattering as possible. A heavy-duty screwdriver I'd left in the drawer seemed to fit the bill. Before launching into my rescue mission, I grabbed a plastic clothing bin from my closet and dumped its contents onto my bed. After setting the bin in the tub, I positioned the vase directly above it to catch all the glass shards as they fell. Given the way Stormy's face was so tightly pressed into the glass at the top, it didn't seem like any shards would reach her if I only broke the bottom.

I wrapped the screwdriver in a hand towel, hoping to keep the breakage to a minimum. Coal sat in the bathroom doorway as if ready to run for help, Lassie-style.

"Here goes nothing," I said, taking a deep breath and pounding into the vase. Nothing happened. I tried again, but the glass didn't even crack. The vase was tougher than I thought. I took the screwdriver from the towel, jamming the metal butt of it into the only bottom section where Stormy's body wasn't directly against the glass.

The vase shattered, and Stormy's body almost dropped onto the shards in the bin. I grabbed her hind end just before she landed. The top part of the vase was unfortunately still intact around her torso, so I'd have to ease her out without cutting her or myself.

Kylie came racing into my room and stopped short behind Coal. "Are you okay?" She took in the bizarre scene.

I sighed. "Yeah. But could you hold her hiney so I can get the rest of her out?"

Coal moved aside, letting Kylie get close. Together, we managed to get Stormy out intact. Once I'd brushed the remaining glass pieces off her long fur, she practically jumped from my arms and shot out of the bathroom as if the floor were on fire.

Kylie sank onto the closed toilet seat. "Wow."

I nodded. "That right there is why I don't have cats." I shrugged. "I like them, but this one in particular is a handful. She belongs to Bo, but I'm not telling him about the stuff she's doing while he's away."

We hadn't told our employees where Bo was going, just that he was taking some of his vacation time and heading south. We didn't explain just *how* south.

"Good idea," Kylie agreed.

I ran down to get couple of heavy duty trash bags to dump the glass into. Chelsea was still sitting at the table, but she stood as I got to the bottom of the steps. "Do you have any containers or bags I can use to put the food away?" she asked.

Shocked at her sudden helpful attitude—and wondering if Kylie had given her a talking-to while I was upstairs—I pointed to the cabinet full of storage containers. She nodded and set about her cleanup task. I grabbed the trash bags and headed back up.

I spoke to Kylie as she worked alongside me. "You're pretty sure that the *exact* sword used to kill Alec was sitting on your table that morning?" I asked, hopeful that she might've sold a similar one long ago.

"I'm positive," she said. "It was one of a kind, and I'd arranged it on the table that morning."

I broached my next topic carefully. "On my way over to the antique cars, I noticed you weren't at your booth. You didn't mention that to Detective Hatcher. Were you gone long?"

She shook her head. "No. It was the weirdest thing. Joel

and I were catching up, then, all of a sudden, I saw this dude in a dark hoodie rushing past. I thought I recognized him, so I told Joel to keep an eye on things. I took off after him to see what he was up to."

I recalled the guy in the dark hoodie bumping into me. "Yeah, I saw that same guy booking it toward the front gate. He was definitely acting weird." I cautiously tried to pick out the few pieces of glass still stuck in the bin. "But who did you think he was? You really should've told the police about him."

"I know. I'll tell Detective Hatcher when he's finished with the house search, but since I never got a good look at the guy's face, I figured it might not even be relevant. I thought the guy was a friend of Alec's named Corey. I don't even know his last name. But I think he sometimes acted as the muscle for some of Alec's underhanded dealings."

"And you didn't think this was relevant?" I demanded. "Kylie, you could've gotten booked for murder! Why didn't you speak up?"

Something flashed in her eyes, and I knew I'd overstepped. "Look," I continued in a calmer tone of voice. "You're one of my favorite baristas, and I can't afford to lose you. So many people trek over to Barks & Beans just to get a latte from you. I don't want to see you throwing everything away just because you're not sure who you saw. Police always want to know the whole story, so who you *think* you saw can be just as important."

"I know, I know," she said. "It's just that I've run into this Corey guy once before—when I was retrieving Chelsea one night, actually—and he's a bad piece of work. The bulked-up type who blindly follows instructions. I don't want someone like that coming after me—or my sister."

"You never know, maybe he'll get put away for murdering his partner in crime," I said.

"Maybe. Anyway, I called Chelsea as soon as I saw it was Alec's body in that car. I had to tell her to watch her back, especially if Corey had anything to do with it," Kylie said. "I don't think he knows where we live, but he does know where Chelsea works. I wanted to make sure she told her manager and kept an eye out for him."

I nodded, tying the bags off. "That was very wise. But how about you call the detective now, just to see how things are going, and you can fill him in." Detective Hatcher needed to know right away that Alec's right-hand man might have been at the flea market on the day Alec was killed. Plus, almost two hours had passed since Kylie and Chelsea came over. Surely the police would've had ample time to search their house...although I assumed they were looking for pills, which could be hidden any number of places.

Kylie stood to her feet. "Do you mind if I talk in your room?"

"No problem." I hauled the bags up and headed downstairs, with Coal trotting down behind me. Chelsea was sitting on the couch, thumbing through her phone. Stormy was perched directly behind her on the top of the couch. She shot me a look that dared me to take one step closer.

"Cheeky kitty," I said.

"What?" Chelsea asked, turning toward me.

"I was just talking to the cat there," I said. As I trekked out the back door to deposit the trash in the garbage bin, Coal barged past me to use the bathroom. "Sorry, boy," I said. I hadn't realized he'd needed to go so urgently. Maybe he was nervous because of our guests or because of the glass vase ordeal with Stormy.

I brought him back in and gave him fresh water before washing my hands at the sink. Kylie trudged downstairs, looking concerned.

"Did you talk to him?" I asked.

Her eyes met mine. "I did. I told him about Corey." She walked over to an armchair in the living room and sat down across from Chelsea.

"And?" I prodded.

"He said that was interesting, but he'd found something even more interesting. There was a vial of GHB liquid in one of my old purses."

"What?!" For once, Chelsea sounded completely in the moment.

Kylie seemed utterly defeated. "Apparently, GHB can also be a liquid. People squirt it in drinks. And somehow, some way, it was in my purse." She shot her sister a look. "Please tell me you didn't know anything about this."

Chelsea looked horrified. "Sis, I promise you I didn't! I'd never want you to go to jail."

Kylie studied her sister for a moment. Her voice softening, she said, "Good. I'm really glad to know that, Chels." She stood and started pacing. "The detective's heading over now to take me into custody. He said the coroner double-checked, and he was able to confirm that Doug's body also had GHB in his system when he died. It's looking like my goose is cooked." Her feet pounded across my wood floorboards.

"No." I leaned across the kitchen counter. "No way. I'm not going to let that happen." Not wanting to divulge the secret of Nels' secret offer, I added, "I know of a really good lawyer, so I'll set that up for you."

Kylie groaned. "I guess I *will* need a lawyer. How much is that going to cost?"

Chelsea piped up. "I'll work extra shifts to help cover it. Besides, they can't keep you in jail for doing nothing, can they?"

Neither Kylie nor I felt like pointing out that the odds were definitely stacked against her. Two men she'd known had been killed with her weapons, and as if that weren't enough, they'd both been drugged beforehand with a liquid found in her possession.

Things had gone from bad to worse in a hurry. Even with a great lawyer at her side, I wasn't sure Kylie was going to be able to dodge this bullet.

14

KYLIE CONTINUED PACING, obviously anxious. "What if the person who planted that vial in my purse comes back? What if they have some kind of way to get into the house?"

Realizing that much of Kylie's worry was over her sister, I offered to have Chelsea stay with me for a little while. After all, I had a guest bedroom, and I no longer feared Chelsea was tangled up in drugs since the police hadn't turned up anything in her bedroom.

Kylie stopped her pacing and gave me an awkward but obviously heartfelt hug. "Thank you," she breathed.

As she sat down on the couch to talk with Chelsea, I unobtrusively grabbed my purse and headed up to my room. I scrounged around in my wallet until I found Nels Hartmann's business card. Unsure how much time I had before the detective showed up, I dropped him a text telling him that Kylie was getting taken into custody and why. Relief poured over me when I got a rapid reply saying he'd let his lawyer know immediately.

True to his word, Detective Hatcher dropped by about

ten minutes later. Kylie pulled Chelsea into a hug, and her younger sister clung to her so tightly, it brought tears to my eyes. If nothing else good came from this, at least Chelsea seemed to have woken up to the reality of how much Kylie loved her.

I sensed reluctance in the detective as he snapped handcuffs on Kylie and escorted her down my solar-lit garden path to the car. Personally, I'd already reached the point where I felt nothing but anger toward whoever had taken such pains to pin two murders on her. Who would hate her so badly that they'd drug people before stabbing them to death with Kylie's weapons, then hide the drug in Kylie's bag? Surely the detective could see how obvious it was that she was being framed.

I pulled him aside as he closed the car door behind Kylie. Hoping the darkness cloaked the disgusted look on my face, I said, "Detective Hatcher, don't you think this is a little too easy? Kylie's weapons were left in the bodies...date-rape drug was left in her purse...how on earth would she even get her hands on that? Besides, why would she shove it in some old purse instead of trashing it after she used it?"

I could just make out the thoughtful look on his face in the light of the street lamp overhead. "Trust me, I'm looking into all the angles, Macy. We do have other suspects. But Kylie jumped to the top of the list with the GHB. We can't ignore evidence like that."

I knew he was only doing his job, and I had to admit that Kylie was in the best hands. Detective Hatcher wasn't like one of those brutal, egotistic cops you saw on TV. If anything, he probably finagled information from people simply by talking to them in his easygoing, down-home style.

It was obvious he took no pleasure in putting Kylie in custody.

As the detective headed over and opened his car door, the interior light came on. I leaned down next to the back window. "I'll look after Chelsea," I mouthed to Kylie.

She nodded, her lips set in a straight line. I hated to see her looking so daunted. She was usually the one employee who was guaranteed to speak up if she felt we were somehow heading in the wrong direction. I truly valued that kind of honesty. But now that she knew the evidence was pointing in the wrong direction—against *her*, no less—she seemed to have lost her fire.

I headed back inside. It was getting late, and the day seemed to have gone on forever. Coal was dozing on the dog bed in the living room, and Chelsea was tucked into the end of the couch, blankly staring ahead.

"You okay?" I asked. "Would you like some herbal tea, or maybe something else to eat?"

She shook her head, causing her thick blonde hair to spill over her shoulders. Glancing at her heavily filled-in eyebrows, I realized with a start that the white hair was probably natural. It seemed unusual that her shade would be so light when Kylie's was so naturally dark. Since their dad's hair was on the dark side, maybe their mom was a natural blonde, but I doubted I'd ever meet her to find out.

Chelsea's white-blonde shade was certainly rare in this neck o' the woods, what with all the dark-haired Scotch-Irish ancestry around. I should know, because Bo and I had gotten picked on plenty of times for our red hair growing up.

I shook off my random musings on hair color. "Let me show you your room," I said, leading Chelsea down the hallway.

Opening the door, I gestured to the queen-sized bed that was covered with one of my favorite fall-colored quilts. "You'll be in here, and there's an attached bathroom. We can drop by your place tomorrow to pick up more clothes while you're staying over."

After glancing around, Chelsea offered me a hesitant smile. It was a heartening thing to see her apathetic armor melting away.

"Thanks," she said. Her brow crinkled. "Honestly, I can't understand what's going on. Why would anyone have an ax to grind against Kylie?"

That was the question I kept asking myself. Who had a motive to frame Kylie?

"Was there anyone who threatened her over the years? Or maybe someone who just bothered her?" I asked.

Chelsea thought a moment. "Well, of course Mom and Dad were mad when she moved me out with her. They're always trying to talk me into coming back, since I'm the baby and all. They swear they've changed and aren't drinking anymore, but Kylie doesn't believe them, so she won't let me leave." She sat on the bed. "Not that I want to, anyway. Dad's probably earning the exact same income as I am at House of Burgers, since he's working at a gas station. And mom doesn't work at all. They really can't afford another mouth to feed, especially with Mom's health issues."

"I'm sorry to hear that," I said.

She shrugged, her face hardened. "Don't be. She brought that mess on herself."

I couldn't imagine feeling that way about your mom, but I hadn't had a mom like that. I'd just had a loving great aunt who'd turned out to be the best mom I ever could have asked for.

"Anyone else?" I asked, feeling fairly certain that Kylie's parents weren't trying to frame her.

"Hm." She rummaged in her mini-backpack, pulling out a phone charger. As she plugged it into the wall, she said, "Well, you've met Joel, right? He's been crazy about her for years. And now he keeps showing up in town, trying to get together with her."

"You don't like him?" I asked, stymied as to what she would have against him. He seemed like a stand-up kind of guy who genuinely liked Kylie.

"I don't," she said. "In fact, I tried to break them up the last time they were together—and it worked."

I recalled how Joel said Chelsea had lied to Kylie, saying he was hitting on her. "What'd you do?" I asked, playing dumb.

"I lied," she admitted. "But I don't regret it. I told Kylie that Joel tried to kiss me. She believed me and dumped him fast."

I leaned into the doorframe. "Chelsea, don't you regret manipulating your sister like that? Wasn't she happy with him?"

She shrugged. "Yeah, she was, but I was younger then. I didn't want to wind up at Mom and Dad's if she and Joel got hitched."

"I doubt Kylie would've left you high and dry," I said.

"I couldn't take that chance." She was dead serious. "So no, I don't regret it."

"But now that Joel's hanging around again, are you still worried they'll get married and leave you behind? Is that why you don't like him?"

She pursed her lips, her gaze shifting toward the quilt. "I don't know. Something about him bugs me, although I have to admit that he really seems to *get* Kylie more than the other guys she's dated."

"Maybe you could just give them a little time and see how things play out," I suggested. I was guessing that the root cause of Chelsea's unease with Joel was directly related to her own fear of being alone. And of all people, I certainly knew how that particular fear could control your life.

As a teen, I'd cried myself to sleep many times after imagining worst-case scenarios with Auntie A, or later, with Bo after he'd joined the Marines. That same fear most likely drove my decision to marry Jake before I'd even had a chance to introduce him to Bo...a mistake I wouldn't make twice. Of course, that was assuming I'd ever reach the point where I'd even *consider* marriage again.

When Chelsea didn't respond to my unsolicited suggestion, I backed out of the room. "Okay, well, you get some sleep. Tomorrow I'll be going to church at eleven, and if you want to come along, you're welcome. Otherwise, please stick around the house until I get back. Then maybe we can walk around town and pick up lunch. There's plenty of cereal and granola bars in the kitchen—just help yourself."

"Thanks," she said. "I'll probably sleep in."

I pulled the door closed, mulling over what she'd told me. Joel didn't seem suspicious enough to be a real suspect, although I'd briefly considered the idea that he might've tried to frame Kylie for murder just to make her feel his pain of being rejected. Still, he'd have to be a total psychopath to go to such extremes to get revenge, and he really didn't strike me that way.

Who else had known about Kylie's attempt to burn Doug's place to the ground? My thoughts roamed as I let Coal out into the backyard a final time.

Bo would have discovered Kylie's criminal history, since he was the one who vetted all our employees when they applied. Obviously, Bo had nothing to do with the murders, but he would've asked Kylie about her conviction for attempted arson before hiring her. Maybe just looking into things from her past had stirred something up.

I began to see how Bo and Kylie's friendship had come about. Bo would have listened to Kylie's explanation of her drastic actions, and, knowing Bo, he'd probably respected her more for trying to bring justice to that old lecher. Both Bo and Kylie were protectors by nature. Although I was sure Kylie had wanted justice for herself, she was also probably trying to protect other girls from Doug...something Emmy Rucker had only wished she could do.

As Coal followed me upstairs, my thoughts shifted toward Emmy. Plain, unassuming Emmy, who'd admitted to celebrating her husband's death. Could she have worked up the courage to inject GHB into Doug's afternoon drink, perhaps? That would've made him easy to stab.

Yet how would she have gotten her hands on a presumably illegal substance? And had she ever bought one of Kylie's knives? She certainly didn't seem the type to frequent weaponry booths.

Besides, she hadn't had any good opportunities to slip the drug vial into Kylie's purse. I knew it hadn't happened the day she visited the cafe, because Kylie always kept her purse tucked into the locked employee drawer in the back room.

In point of fact, Emmy seemed *grateful* to Kylie, not likely to frame her.

Nothing was adding up.

I buttoned up one of the worn Oxford cloth shirts that had belonged to my dad. Auntie A had given some of his shirts to me when I was a teen, and they had become my all-time favorite loungewear. I appreciated the tangible connection to him, and besides, the cotton always seemed just the right weight, no matter what the temperature was in the house.

I snuggled under the covers while Coal set to work kneading his pillow at the foot of my bed. I couldn't think of anyone who would've known of Kylie's attempt on Doug's life *and* wanted to frame her for murder. But maybe I hadn't met enough people in Kylie's circle of friends yet?

I let out a dubious puff of air. Kylie's circle of friends seemed limited to the people she hung out with at the Ren Faire and her fellow employees at Barks & Beans. No one in the cafe had anything against her, and the only person from the Ren Faire who'd been around was Joel, whose sole intent seemed to be winning Kylie over.

As far as our customers went, no one had complained about Kylie—if anything, they'd preferred her over the other baristas, at least until she'd been connected with Alec's murder. I couldn't imagine anyone getting so disgruntled over a botched latte order that they'd go out and kill two people.

No, there had to be someone I wasn't aware of. I yawned and flipped off my night table lamp. Maybe I'd have a clearer head in the morning. Coal's gentle snores lulled me into a much-needed sleep.

15

CHELSEA'S BEDROOM door was still closed as I got ready for church in the morning. When Summer dropped by to pick me up, I got in her car and explained what had happened after work yesterday.

Although she didn't say a word, the dubious look on her face told me she wasn't entirely convinced of Kylie's innocence.

"Come on, Summer," I said. "You can't really believe that Kylie drugged and stabbed those men."

Her lips pursed. "Well, if there's one thing I've learned from hanging around you and your brother, it's that anyone is capable of anything, given the right set of circumstances. I mean, just think of the murderers you've run into who've been living right under our noses. Besides, are you forgetting that Kylie once tried to burn Doug's house down around him? Maybe she went back to finish the job. She could've felt she had some legit reason to rid the world of Alec Marchand, too."

"I've definitely considered what you're suggesting, but it

doesn't add up. Why on earth would Kylie leave the murder weapons out where cops would be sure to find them?"

Summer pulled into the church parking lot. She pulled down the visor mirror to touch up her lipstick, then turned to me. "Yeah, I guess you're right. While I have no doubt that Kylie could be quite the calculated murderer if she felt the need for it, I also have no doubt she'd plan things out a whole lot better than this."

"That's quite the vote of confidence for Kylie," I said, laughing. "But I agree."

Her brown eyes were tinged with concern. "What's going to happen to her sister if she has to go to prison? It sounds like she can't really go back to her parents."

I took a deep breath. "We'll cross that bridge when we come to it. For now, I'm the one keeping an eye on Chelsea, and so far, she doesn't seem to hate me for it."

Summer squeezed my arm. "No one could hate you, Macy. And speaking of your adoring fans, have you figured out how long Jake the Snake is staying in town?"

It was amusing that my friend had adopted my own nickname for my ex—a moniker that was sadly grounded on cold, hard facts. "The Snake" was a constant reminder of what he'd done to me.

"I have no idea, but I'm actively ignoring him at this point," I said. "He texted me after the cafe celebration to ask how it went, but I never answered him."

She nodded. "Good girl. Let him guess."

I shook my head. "He also texted that he's still in town, in case I wanted to get together again. That's just getting pretty ridiculous. Isn't his dad concerned about showing Jake the ropes of owning the dealership before he retires?"

Summer pulled her long hair out of her collar, letting it

cascade across her shoulders. She rarely put her hair in a ponytail for church. "I don't know, but I'm telling you, he probably won't leave town until you tell him goodbye—in person."

"By that time, maybe it'll come out more like *get lost*," I said.

She grinned as she opened the car door. "Maybe that'll be just the ticket."

CHURCH RAN A LITTLE LATE, making me more and more anxious to get home and make sure Chelsea hadn't flown the coop. Although she'd seemed seriously rattled by the events of last night, I wasn't sure I could trust her to stay put. Of course, she didn't have a car, but it didn't take long to get anywhere in town on foot...and I feared she still had some unsavory acquaintances around.

But as I walked into the house and Coal met me at the door, I was pleased to find Chelsea relaxing on the couch stroking Stormy, who sat purring in her lap. Bo's cat had truly taken quite a shine to my guest.

"Hey there," I said. "You getting hungry?"

Chelsea gave me a lazy grin. "I actually just ate a granola bar about fifteen minutes ago. I'm okay."

Feeling generous since Chelsea hadn't betrayed my trust and run off, I said, "I was thinking about taking a walk in town, maybe over to my friend's art gallery? And we could pick up some lunch, too?"

Chelsea perked up, her light blue eyes meeting mine. "Sure, that sounds great."

After I'd gotten Coal and Stormy squared away, I

grabbed the keys and motioned for Chelsea to follow. It was the perfect kind of day outside, with silver-shadowed clouds and the kind of gentle, white-tinged sunlight that didn't overheat the pavement. I hoped the gorgeous day was a reflection of how things were going with Kylie at the police station. I knew she'd get in touch with me the first chance she could.

Dylan's gallery was busy, which was great to see. I glanced around, impressed to see that The Discerning Palette was becoming a kind of tourist destination. I hardly recognized any of the customers as locals.

The gallery was light and airy, as one would expect, with minimalist furniture precisely situated here and there. Chelsea was drawn to three large portraits near the front, which I instantly recognized as the work of Dylan's artist protégé.

Dylan's assistant, Shanda, walked my way. "Hello, Miss Hatfield. And to what do we owe the pleasure of having you here today? Are you looking for something in particular?"

I smiled at the perky, dark-haired woman, who was about twenty years my senior. "I'm not planning to buy today, thank you. I just brought a friend over to see your gorgeous artwork." I gestured toward Chelsea, who didn't quite look the art gallery type in her ripped-up jeans and holey black T-shirt.

Shanda, bless her, didn't pay one bit of attention to Chelsea's attire. Instead, she walked directly to her side and gave her a warm welcome. I made a mental note to tell Dylan to give her a raise.

I wandered closer to the sculptures on display between the paintings. As I leaned closer to examine a curving white piece that vaguely resembled driftwood, Dylan's voice sounded behind me.

"Pretty, isn't it? Believe it or not, it's concrete, but it looks almost like marble, doesn't it?"

I turned and smiled, allowing myself a moment to appreciate just how well put-together my gallery owner friend was. His brown, tousled hair just touched the collar of his navy blazer. The dark blue eyes behind his glasses held a special twinkle for me. His cleft chin was reminiscent of the greats of black and white Hollywood. He looked exactly like what he was—an artsy, well-read guy who was friendly, but no pushover.

And, as Summer kept pointing out, he was obviously into me. I'd felt attracted to him from the moment we'd met, and since then, we'd gotten more and more comfortable with each other. While I was certain that close friendship was the goal of any solid relationship, I'd never before experienced one where the zing factor gave way to a steady friendship. Was that what I should be looking for, or something else?

Chelsea walked over to my side, her gaze traveling from Dylan to me. "Hey," she said, nudging my elbow.

"Hey." Snapping out of my pensive mode, I made introductions. When Chelsea expressed interest in the portraits, Dylan was only too happy to share the stories that inspired the artwork. I trailed behind them as they walked over to examine them more closely. I had to admit, it was endearing to see Dylan explain brushstroke techniques to a girl who likely had no sweet clue what he was talking about and no means to purchase a painting. For some reason, it was like I was seeing Dylan in a new light today, and that light was definitely golden.

Chelsea moseyed over to look at the sculptures, so I

stepped closer and spoke to Dylan. "It's great to see your business is booming," I said. "But I know it's not by accident. I've seen how hard you work on marketing."

He nodded, excited as a little boy. "I'm so glad I found this artist—I really believe he's going to become famous one day. I don't even have to talk his pieces up. They sell themselves." He glanced around. "I should probably get over to my customers," he said ruefully. "Oh, hey, a blond guy came in this morning and he got to talking about Barks & Beans. Said he knew someone who worked there. I wondered if he meant you. He seemed friendly enough."

My teeth clenched. Jake had probably been trolling around town, gathering info on me. Had he discovered I'd been dating Dylan, then hunted down his place of business to spy on him?

"Did he say anything else?" I asked.

Dylan thought for a moment. "Oh, yes, he mentioned that he's not in town for long. He's camping over by Moncove Lake, I think."

Wait a second. That wasn't Jake.

"Did he have glasses?" I asked.

Dylan nodded, his look curious. "Do you know him?"

"I sure do." It had to be Joel Fuller. He hadn't headed back to North Carolina yet. Which meant he'd lied to Kylie when he told her that he was leaving yesterday.

But why?

"Thanks for letting me know," I said. "Well, we'd better get rolling. Thanks for talking with Chelsea about the paintings." I leaned closer to him. "I could tell she enjoyed it, and she's pretty tough to impress."

He gave me a wink, a smile playing at his lips. "I was happy to. Hey, would you happen to be free any time this week? I was thinking maybe we could go for a walk on the trail."

The Greenbrier River trail was a former railroad that had been transformed into a wide pathway where people could walk, bike, or even ride horses along the river. It was a beautiful trek, and I was drawn to the idea of hanging out in nature with Dylan, since we hadn't done that much.

"Sure. Maybe Friday after work? I'll let you know how things are looking," I said.

After saying goodbye to Dylan, I walked over and retrieved Chelsea from the back of the gallery. Once we were out on the sidewalk, she turned to me and gave an exhilarated sigh. "He's ultra attractive. Like, 'sir, who decided you could look that good' attractive."

I chuckled. "Yes, without a doubt." Although I was pleased to see Chelsea expanding her playing field to include guys of an upstanding nature, I knew Dylan wasn't interested in girls her age. "Listen, I just thought of an errand I need to run—would you mind if we headed back and did drive-through for lunch?"

"Oh, sure. Or if you have chicken and rice, I can whip up a casserole. I don't have many recipes in my arsenal, but Kylie taught me an easy one for nights I was home alone."

I cut a side glance at her, once again surprised at the hidden depths in Kylie's once-petulant younger sister.

"That's sweet of you. How about this—we can order delivery. Your choice. Then you don't have to cook, and I can head out and get my errand done."

"That'll be great."

We walked in companionable silence until we reached the house. After letting Coal out, I ran up to my room and tucked the serrated pocketknife Bo had given me into my front jeans pocket. I wasn't entirely sure my "errand" was going to play out in a safe fashion, but I knew I couldn't risk taking Chelsea along. If things went south and Chelsea got hurt, Kylie would find a way to kill me—whether she was in jail or not.

It would take me about forty-five minutes to get where I was going, so I told Chelsea to go ahead and eat when the food arrived. I didn't plan to linger, so I said she could expect me back in about three hours, tops.

Then I got in my car and texted Summer that if I didn't text her back by four, she was to call Detective Hatcher to let him know what I was doing and give him my location.

I should've known her response would be immediate—and irate. She called me up, her normally even keel shot to pieces. "What do you think you're *doing*? You are *not* going there alone, or your brother would hit the roof. I'm going with you, no questions asked."

"But it's your day off—"

"I don't *care* what day it is. You pick me up." She hung up.

I drove off, secretly thankful Summer had volunteered to tag along. Most likely, my trip would come to nothing. But on the off-chance that it did blow up in my face, it was a relief to know someone would be there for me.

16

MONCOVE LAKE WAS JUST as I remembered from the numerous times Auntie A had taken us there. Bo and I would swim for hours in the lake, then come in for hot dogs straight off the charcoal grill. I still vividly remembered the time Bo swam over and punched an older teen who had made some inappropriate remarks to me, even though I was wearing an extremely modest swimsuit.

I drove around the camping area, looking for a car with a North Carolina plate. Although Joel could've moved into a hotel by now, I sensed he was the kind of guy who liked roughing it, Ren Faire style.

Driving onto a side road, I caught sight of a silver truck parked near a tent. As I slowed down, Summer confirmed that the truck was from North Carolina.

I pulled to a stop along the roadside and opened my door. Summer jumped out and raced around to join me. She'd already forcefully declared that she wasn't letting me walk up to an isolated campsite on my own.

There was no one in sight as we neared the clearing. "Hello?" I shouted.

Something rustled in the tent, then the zipper slid down. Joel stepped out in his pajama bottoms. His curls were mashed up against the side of his head. He wasn't wearing glasses and was staring at us like he couldn't quite make out who we were.

"Joel, it's Macy Hatfield—Kylie's friend," I said. "And this is my friend, Summer. I just wanted to ask you a couple of questions, if you don't mind."

Recognition dawned, and he offered us a smile. "Oh, sure. You can have a seat over at the picnic table. I'll just grab my glasses really quick."

He ducked back into the tent. I held my breath, hoping he wasn't going to burst out with a weapon in hand. It didn't make sense why he'd stuck around town, even after Kylie had gotten hauled into jail.

He returned quickly, glasses squarely planted on his face. He took a seat across from us. "Hi, Macy. I'm glad to see you again. Sorry I wasn't exactly ready for visitors. I didn't get much sleep last night, so I was taking a little siesta. What can I do for you?"

I could almost feel Summer's eyes boring into him, so I shot her a sideways look to dial it back. I hadn't even talked to the poor guy yet. "I was just wondering why you hadn't gone back to North Carolina, since that's what Kylie told me you were planning," I said.

He shrugged, his expression hurt. "I didn't think she really cared what I did." He flicked a ladybug off the table. "I decided to stay another night since I'd already made the trip. But some crazy owl kept hooting above me all night long, so let's just say things weren't as relaxing as I'd planned."

"I'm sorry." I returned to my primary objective. "Joel, you've probably bought some of Kylie's weapons over the years, right?"

His eyes narrowed. "Sure I have. But I didn't buy the kind you might be wondering about." He stiffened, his eyes shifting between Summer and me. "Tell me again why you two came all the way out here."

Ignoring him, I asked, "And Kylie didn't *give* you any weapons?"

Joel's lips curled. "Are you insinuating that I killed one of those guys? The police have already talked to me. What possible motive would I have?"

That was what I was trying to find out, but I couldn't come out and say *that*. Maybe I'd taken the wrong approach.

I softened my tone. "Did you know they took Kylie into custody yesterday night?" I watched his reaction to see if he looked happy that his frame job had worked or if he seemed genuinely sad.

Instead, he merely looked bewildered. "Why? I thought they didn't have any evidence against her."

I was the one asking the questions here. "They found something directly related to the murders," I said vaguely. Frustrated that I couldn't get anything out of him, I gave Summer a desperate look. We'd discussed Joel's possible motive for framing Kylie on the way over, so maybe she'd come up with some unique approach to questioning.

Taking my lead, she folded her hands and leaned in toward Joel. Thumbing her nose at her peace-loving Mennonite upbringing, she went straight for the jugular and asked, "I'll bet you were crushed when Kylie rejected you...again. How did you deal with it?"

He gaped, but managed to blurt out his answer. "You

really want to know how it hit me? Well, I'll tell you. I left the cafe and headed straight back to camp. I picked up a greasy meatball sub, a giant slushy drink, and a couple of Snoball cakes from the gas station, then I sat down by the lake and ate until I was stuffed. Then I wrote some lame poetry and wished I'd never fallen in love with Kylie Rosalind Baer."

I wasn't sure which was more shocking—hearing his admission of love, or finding out that Kylie had such a gorgeous middle name.

It really seemed that Joel was telling us the truth. The poor guy looked like he'd been run through the wringer and had barely made it out alive. There was no need for us to continue grilling this broken young man, so I gave Summer's hand a light tap. "Well, we'd better get going. Thank you for talking with us, Joel. We're sorry to bother you."

"Would you let me know how things go with her?" he asked. "I still don't understand what evidence they could have found. Kylie wouldn't have killed those men. Sure, she didn't like Alec—she told me that many times—but she wouldn't have killed him just because he was dating her sister."

I stood, working my way off of the picnic bench. "Did Kylie ever mention Doug Rucker in all the years you've known her?"

He walked over toward his dead campfire, picking up a long stick to poke at the coals. "Not by name. But from what Emmy said, I gathered Doug was the man Kylie told me about when we were dating. I'd asked her about the meaning behind her dragon tattoo—if it was like the girl in those books. She said the dragon represented power, and even though some old dude had once stolen that from her, she would never allow anyone to take that from her again. I gotta say it sounded intimidating, but at that moment, I knew I didn't care if she wanted to rule my entire life." He jabbed at a coal. "I'm hopeless, right?"

I grinned, unable to resist his honest spirit. "No, Joel. I actually think you might be just right for Kylie. She needs someone who's willing to risk it all for her. Are you in a hurry to head back to North Carolina?"

"Yeah. Even though I'm able to work remotely, the campsite has spotty coverage. I was planning to drive down tonight."

I threw Summer my keys. Getting the message that I wanted to talk to Joel alone, she gave him a polite nod and strolled toward my vehicle.

Joel's curious eyes met mine as I stepped closer to him. "Listen, you can't give up yet," I said. "I have a feeling Kylie's going to get out of this—we both know she didn't murder those men. But she's going to need someone who can help her work through things. Obviously, her parents don't give a hoot about her, and although everyone at the cafe will support her, we're not as close to her as you are. These murders have opened a chapter in her life she thought she'd closed, and she's probably feeling weaker than she has in a long time. If you are there for her, I do believe you'll win her trust."

Joel dipped his head. "I won't give up," he said quietly. "I want her to know I'm always there for her."

"I'm glad to hear that," I said. "Give me your number, and I'll let you know the moment things take any kind of turn."

After Joel and I swapped numbers, I headed over to the SUV. As I climbed in, Summer gave me a proud look. "So, what'd you think about my interview technique?"

"Dangerous," I said. "Remind me not to get on your bad side. You'd gut me like a fish."

She laughed. "I only save that approach for possible criminals. You have nothing to fear."

Our gazes were drawn to the placid lake as we drove by. While I was glad that Joel hadn't stuck around for the nefarious purpose of killing Doug, I also wished I hadn't come to a dead end in regard to helping Kylie. The detective had assured me he was looking into other suspects, but now his entire focus was necessarily on Kylie...which left someone out there who'd killed before and might find a reason to do it again.

I pulled up to Summer's apartment, which was a large, renovated space over an older couple's garage. Her rental arrangement worked out well, since Mr. and Mrs. Maynard allowed cats, and Summer was continually fostering them. Not to mention, she was able to use her green thumb to maintain their gardens each summer, and in return, they knocked some off her rent.

"How are the Maynards doing?" I asked.

She rolled her eyes. "Fighting, as usual. I've never seen anyone scrap around as much as those two. He says plant the tulip bulbs; she says plant hyacinths instead. He says they're going on a cruise; she says they're taking a train trip. It's insane."

"And yet he still buys her roses every Saturday and they waltz the night away, right?"

Summer gave a bewildered nod. "Love. Ain't it grand."

I PULLED up to my curb and got out, hurrying toward my gate. I was dying to find out how Waffles was adjusting to her new abode with Vera, but I'd have to wait for a better time to drop by. I hadn't eaten lunch, and now it was nigh on toward supper time. I was running through meal ideas when I unlocked the back door and nearly opened it into Coal, who was planted right behind it.

I patted his head. "What are you doing, boy?" The delicious aromas of herbed tomatoes, pasta, and fresh bread wafted through the house. Although a pot simmered on the stove, I didn't see my houseguest anywhere.

"Chelsea?" I called out.

Stormy obediently raced to my side, as if I'd called her personally. I picked her up, stroking her long fur. "How are you doing, little honey? You like Chelsea, don't you?"

Chelsea walked down the hallway, and I had to grin. She wore my ruffled red gingham apron, and her long hair was tossed up into a bun. With her dark eyeliner, she looked like a housewife from the fifties.

"Sorry, I had to grab my phone. Don't worry, I'm making supper," she said. "Although there's leftover pizza if you want some. I got the supreme."

"Good choice," I said. "But whatever you're cooking smells amazing. I'd love to have that."

"I found some yeast rolls in your freezer," she said. "And I made up my own spaghetti sauce. We'll see how it turned out."

"I'll wash my hands and make a salad," I offered.

"How'd your errand go?" she asked, her back to me as she stirred the pot.

"It was...productive, I guess." I wanted to tell Chelsea

that Joel really did care for her sister, but I decided not to bring it up. "Did anything happen while I was gone?"

After checking the rolls, she turned toward me. "Well, let's just say your dog snores like a freight train when he naps. But he *is* super sweet and obedient. I let him out a couple of times, and he came right up to the porch when I called him in."

"Good boy," I said, and Coal thumped his tail against my leg.

A loud electric guitar tune ripped through the air. It took me a second to realize it was Chelsea's phone, which she picked up.

"Hey. What? Oh, good! Hang on—I'll let you talk to her." Chelsea handed me the phone, mouthing the word "Kylie."

"I got out on bail." Kylie sounded weary. "Would you be able to pick me up?"

"Of course! Did the lawyer get you out?" I asked.

"No, but thanks for calling him in. Last night I actually had to go before the judge before the lawyer even got there, but it turns out that's standard procedure. Even though the detective told the judge I wasn't a flight risk, he still set the bail high, so I assumed I'd be in jail for a long time. Today they interrogated me, and my lawyer sat in on that." She gave a small yawn. "But then tonight, the detective said someone posted my bail, so he's letting me out. I can't believe it." Her voice wavered.

I assumed Nels had anonymously posted Kylie's bail, so I didn't ask any questions. "Okay. I'll be over in about ten minutes, okay?"

"Sounds great."

As I was slipping my shoes on, the doorbell rang, sending Coal into a flurry of barking. "Hush, boy," I commanded.

Pulling him into a sitting position at my side, I opened the door. I didn't recognize the beefy, heavily bearded man standing on the doorstep. His bleary eyes shifted to Coal, then back to my face.

"Is Chelsea here?" he asked, his words slurred.

Coal took a small step forward. There was no way he was letting this guy in the house.

"Who are you?" I asked, fingering the flip-out knife that was still in my pocket.

"Name's Corey," he said. "I knew her boyfriend real well."

"She's not—"

Chelsea edged up behind me. "Corey, get lost."

He leered at her, revealing numerous missing teeth. I recognized it as "meth mouth," the severe tooth decay experienced by methamphetamine users. "I'm not gettin' lost until you hand over the stuff," he said. "I know Alec gave it to you before he kicked it." As he took a stumbling step toward her, Coal jumped to his feet and stood at attention, the hair down his back bristling. He gave a growl that said he meant business.

Thankfully, Corey had the good sense to pay attention and back up. He glared at Chelsea, who was still safely tucked behind Coal. "No good's gonna come of this," he spat out. "I got people waiting on that stuff and I plan to get it. You better watch your step." He wheeled around and stomped down the stairs. I watched until he went out my gate, letting it slam behind him.

I shut and locked the door, leaning against it. Chelsea gave a little screech as the smell of burning rolls hit us. She rushed over to the oven, grabbed a potholder, and yanked them out.

After flipping them onto a pan, she said, "Only the bottoms were burned. Sorry about that."

The rolls were the least of our worries. Chelsea had just become a target for a drug dealer, and she needed to explain why.

17

I HATED to put Chelsea on the spot, but Kylie needed to know what kind of situation she was walking into with Corey on the loose. After covering the rolls and turning the sauce off so we could run over to pick up Kylie, I asked Chelsea some direct questions.

"When Corey said you had Alec's stuff, I take it he meant drugs," I said. "Did Alec give you anything to hold onto?"

She shook her head, pulling her shoes on. "No way. I told him I didn't want a thing to do with any of that stuff."

I sighed as I grabbed my purse. "But why on earth did you date someone like that in the first place?"

Chelsea opened the back door, ready to head to the SUV. "I don't know. I mean, he was handsome and rich, and he bought me all kinds of nice things. He always told me how beautiful I was."

"But you knew how he got all that money. How could you stomach it?" I followed her out, making sure I'd locked my door in case Corey decided to pay a return visit.

Her tone took on an edge. "I don't know, okay? I can't explain it. He was just there for me."

I was sure he was, probably for his own underhanded purposes. I was guessing he might have even planned on using Chelsea as a drug runner at some point, since she'd be far less likely to be picked up.

Hopefully after all this mess cleared up, Chelsea would actually listen to her sister's advice about who she shouldn't date.

After a quick drive to the police station, we parked and walked inside. It didn't take long for Kylie to greet us, looking much the worse for wear with dark circles under her eyes. Just outside my SUV, after standing in silence a moment, Kylie reached over and gave Chelsea a long hug. Then she gave me one, too.

"Thank you so much, Miss Hatfield. I can't thank you enough for being there for Chelsea. I knew I didn't have to worry about her."

I gave her a halfhearted smile. Unfortunately, thanks to Corey's sudden appearance, Kylie would have something new to worry about. Realizing I needed to report his visit to Detective Hatcher, I asked the sisters to wait in the vehicle while I ran inside.

After I explained that I needed to tell my friend Charlie Hatcher something, the lady at the desk called him over. Detective Hatcher's steely gray stubble had grown in, and he, too, looked tired. "Macy," he said. "How can I help you? Is your friend out?"

"She is," I said. "And thank you for telling the judge she wasn't a flight risk, by the way. I'll be taking her home later tonight, but I needed to report an incident to you first. A guy named Corey came to my house and threatened Chelsea

Baer. He believes she's got Alec Marchand's drugs somewhere, but she swears she doesn't. Since you've searched her place, I'm sure you'd agree that she doesn't have them. I'm worried about those sisters living alone...what if he shows up at their house? They don't have a huge guard dog like I do."

He nodded. "We've been trying to track Corey down. Did you see what car he was driving?"

"No—I just watched to make sure he left my back yard, then I heard him pull out."

He looked thoughtful. "Although it's a little unorthodox to send a patrol car out to a house of someone who just got out of jail, I can see your point. Chelsea has become a target, for whatever reason. I don't have unlimited resources, as you know, but I'm not going to stand by and let this guy terrorize them. I'll have an officer drive by their place a couple of times a day until we can find Corey."

"Thank you so much," I said, fighting the urge to give him a hug. Detective Hatcher was the kind of police officer who restored my trust in humanity.

"Too bad your brother's not in town," he added. "This drug network stuff is right up his alley."

He was right. Bo's DEA background would've enabled him to track down a dealer like Corey in no time flat. I sighed. "Yeah, Corey would've had an entirely different experience if Bo had been at my house today. I definitely miss having him around."

The detective gave me a knowing look. "What he's working on now is going to make a long-term difference in West Virginia. The Alecs and the Coreys of this state are going to feel a whole new type of pain if Bo succeeds."

I didn't want to think what could happen if he *didn't*

succeed. "Thank you," I said quietly, and headed out the door.

As we ate our late spaghetti supper, I told Kylie about Corey's visit. Chelsea looked on gloomily, as if she wanted to disassociate herself from her troublesome dating past. Her remorse was definitely a step in the right direction.

Coal seemed to take on an emotional support dog role, leaning against Kylie when she sat down on the couch and making whiney sounds up at her, like he felt her pain. His eyes looked so concerned, I got the feeling he could sense every bit of Kylie's hurt. As for Kylie, she barely stopped petting him, as if he offered some kind of lifeline.

When I dropped the women off at their house, I felt certain that Kylie would head straight for her weapons supply to make sure they were armed to the teeth, at least until the police pulled Corey off the streets. I advised Kylie to take tomorrow off work and get caught up on sleep. She agreed and said she was going to have Chelsea take the day off, too. "He knows where she works, so it's not worth the risk," Kylie said. "Hopefully the detective will find him quickly."

"He'll make it a priority," I said. "Call me if you need anything—even in the night."

"Thanks so much, and you lock up well, too," Kylie warned. "He might try to come back to your place."

As I got into my SUV, a shiver raced up my arms. Of course I had Coal, and he wouldn't let Corey into the house. But now Corey *knew* I had Coal...so what if he shot him first, then barged upstairs? I'd have to be ready for that possibility, so that meant I'd need to get out the .22 rifle Bo had given me years ago. I was comfortable with the gun, since Bo often had me practice with it.

A question that had occurred to me earlier resurfaced. How in the world had Corey discovered that Chelsea was staying at my place? Had someone been stalking Chelsea...or even me?

Something told me I wouldn't be sleeping well tonight.

MONDAY MORNING FELT every bit like a Monday when my alarm buzzed. It was pouring rain out, and the house had turned chilly overnight. I scrounged in my winter clothes bin and found a cornflower-blue turtleneck sweater that was a staple in colder months. I recalled how Jake had told me it made my gray-blue eyes look even bluer, then shoved aside that intrusive thought.

Coal balked at going out into the rain, but I forced him to use the bathroom, knowing he couldn't wait until I got home. After one of his fastest runs ever, he returned to the porch and let me rub him down with an old towel before letting him in. It was amazing how much mud his huge paws could pick up in such a short time.

I retrieved several cat toys from under the couch and dropped them around in the living room for Stormy to enjoy. She rewarded me by rubbing against my leg, purring.

Unwilling to make a dash through the pouring rain, I unlocked the connecting door and headed into the cafe. Days like this, I was grateful that Bo had bought his own place so I could live in the back section of Auntie A's. Although the cafe was spacious, I had plenty of room in the other half of the three-story building I'd called home for so long.

Charity and Bristol arrived soon after I did. Today, Bristol would be working the cafe while I was in the Barks section. Summer came in next and dropped off a couple of dogs, and from her monosyllabic answers, I knew she hadn't gotten much sleep. I figured she'd probably experienced late-night cat problems of one type or another.

The dismal weather seemed to deter customers, although a few of our regulars showed up. Each time someone came in, I had to race over to the entryway, mopping up the water they'd sloshed in.

When Charity took an early lunch break, Bristol edged out from behind the coffee bar to stand near the gas fireplace. I rubbed at my arms, which felt chilled even in my sweater. Today was one of those days I wished Bo could've installed a fireplace in the Barks section, but given the unpredictability of the shelter dogs, I knew that was impossible. It would only take one rambunctious dog to go crashing into it and light the place up.

A lady in a raincoat and one of those older plastic scarf-style rain hats stepped in. Her boots—which could only have been termed *galoshes*—dripped onto the floor. Grabbing the mop and a towel, I hurried over to clean things up behind her as she unknotted her scarf.

She blinked up at me and I realized it was Emmy Rucker. We hadn't been properly introduced, so I tried not to let on that I recognized her. "Hello, and welcome to Barks & Beans," I said. "I'm the owner, Macy Hatfield, and I hope you enjoy your visit. It's messy out there, isn't it?"

She gave an impassive nod. Throwing an anxious glance toward the coffee bar, she asked, "Is Kylie working today?"

"I'm afraid not. But Bristol is a skilled barista, as well."

Emmy's face fell. "Thank you, but I didn't come for the coffee. I read in the paper that Kylie got taken into custody, and I needed to see for myself. Is that true? Is she going to jail?"

I could tell she was getting worked up, so I tried to reassure her. "She was taken into custody, yes, but she's out now." I didn't add that she'd gotten out on bail.

The woman wrung her hands and eased into a nearby chair. "Oh, my. This isn't what was supposed to happen. Did they have some kind of evidence against her? The poor dear!"

I wasn't sure how much to tell Emmy. Although she did seem genuinely concerned for Kylie, I knew she also happened to be Doug's widow. If she'd killed him, she could be probing for information, hoping against hope that Kylie would take the fall for the murder of her nasty husband.

"I really can't tell you much, but obviously they didn't find enough to keep her," I said.

Emmy bobbed her head. "Good. That's good." A quizzical look crossed her face. "But I still just don't understand it."

One of the shelter dogs started licking at the dog gate and whining. "Unfortunately, I think it's time for a doggie bathroom break," I said, dreading the rainy chore ahead of me. "Thank you for dropping by, and please don't worry about Kylie. I think she's going to be okay."

She offered a forced smile. "I do hope so." She stood, giving her plastic scarf a light shake before tying it neatly beneath her chin. "Please tell her that Emmy dropped in and asked after her."

"I will," I said. As I walked over to the Barks section, I tried to understand why Emmy was so invested in what happened to Kylie. Was she genuinely concerned about a woman she respected for standing up to her husband? Or was she motivated by something more sinister?

While I was snapping leashes on the dogs' collars, Emmy's words played in my mind. She'd said "This isn't what was supposed to happen."

What *was* supposed to happen?

18

As the day wore on, the rain didn't let up, so our customer flow didn't improve. Charity headed out to pick up her grandson from preschool. Bristol's dark head stayed bent over her phone, and I knew she was researching colleges with the best Graphic Design programs. Barks & Beans was going to lose her next fall and I didn't look forward to it, but Bo and I planned to make a substantial anonymous donation toward her further education. Bristol had worked for years to help her single mom make ends meet for their small family, and now we wanted to make sure she got the chance to achieve her dream.

Just before closing time, Summer dropped in to pick up the dogs. She was looking decidedly more perky at this hour. "Any takers on these two?" she asked. "No one came to the shelter to fill out paperwork, but I was hoping maybe they just didn't get over there?"

I shook my head. "We hardly had any customers, although someone interesting did pay a visit." I shared about my conversation with Emmy, hoping to get Summer's take on it.

She cocked her head. "You're right, that's weird. Is she for Kylie or against her? And like you say, what was supposed to happen with her husband's death?"

"I could ask Kylie what she's thinking about Emmy, although she really seemed to like her, talking about what a great teacher she used to be."

"Well, sometimes life changes people in bad ways," Summer said bleakly.

I had a feeling her comment was coming from personal experience, but from the closed look on her face, I could tell she didn't want to talk about it. Summer rarely shared anything from her childhood. I knew that she'd grown up in a Mennonite community and that she had four brothers and no sisters, but that was about the size of it. I wondered how much she'd opened up to Bo about that side of her life.

Summer took the dogs and left, and Bristol headed out soon after. I had just locked the front door when someone tried the handle, then started pounding on it.

Fearing it was Corey, I raced to the coffee bar and found a knife. Gripping it tightly, I returned to the door and did a quick peek out the front window.

It was Kylie, her wet hair plastered against her head.

I hurried to let her in. "Hey there—you're so wet! What's going on?"

"I've just gotten some horrible news and I wanted to talk with you about it," Kylie said. "I grabbed Chelsea and raced over here, hoping to catch you before you left work."

"You walked over?" I asked, incredulous.

"Oh, no, I drove, but I had to park up the street and I forgot my umbrella. But listen—Detective Hatcher just texted to tell me that Emmy Rucker had a bad wreck. They found her car rammed into a tree on the opposite side of the road." She took a deep breath. "She was killed in the crash."

I had to sit down. "But I just saw her today."

Kylie sat down next to me, water dripping onto the floor beneath her. "What do you mean? She came here?"

"She did. She was asking about you, actually. She said to be sure to tell you that she'd looked in on you. She seemed really concerned that you'd been taken into custody." I gave her a quick recount of Emmy's visit.

Kylie crossed her arms and shivered, obviously cold and distraught. "It seems like the crash was a random coincidence, but do you really think it was? The detective said he was letting me know because they still haven't been able to locate Corey. Does that mean he suspects Corey had something to do with it?"

"Sounds like it," I said. "And I think the detective is concerned about you and your sister."

"I hope that means he's ruled me out as a suspect in the murders," Kylie said.

"Unfortunately, just because you made bail doesn't mean you aren't a suspect anymore," I said. "Until they find the actual murderer, I'm afraid you'll still be closely watched."

"I don't care about that," Kylie said. "My life is basically an open book at this point. They already know my criminal history, limited as it is. I just want everything to go back to normal for Chelsea and me."

"Do you think she has any idea where Corey would hang out?" I asked. "I'm sure the police have asked her, but maybe you could encourage her to think about any of the places she's run into him in the past."

"I'll do that," Kylie said. She rubbed her hands up and

down her wet arms. "I'd better go home and dry off. I just wanted to let you know. I can't understand what's going on."

I stood, walking her to the door. "I don't, either. Although we've had nonstop rain all day, so it's possible some of the roads were flooded. It would've been easy for Emmy to skid across and hit a tree, especially if her visibility was limited due to fog or even something like junky wiper blades. I've nearly wrecked on the mountain myself when I hydroplaned in weather like this."

"Me, too," Kylie said.

I gave her arm a light squeeze. "Get home and get warmed up," I said. "And please be careful."

Her hazel eyes sparked. "Oh, don't you worry. I'm on the alert, now more than ever."

"Good." As she ran up the sidewalk, I headed back in to lock up. Everything seemed to be happening at once. In a little over a week, three people had died, two with murder weapons sticking out of them. At least none of Kylie's weapons had been found in Emmy Rucker's body, which would seem to back the idea that her death was accidental.

Poor Emmy. She had just been freed from a loveless marriage to a man who should've been locked up years ago for his crimes against women. Now, instead of being able to pursue her own dreams again, Emmy lost her life, way too soon.

My phone rang, startling me. Glancing at the screen, I saw that it was the number Bo had called me from the last time. A smile spread across my face as I picked up.

"Hey there, bro!"

Bo's familiar voice seemed to wipe away all my despondent thoughts. "Hey, Macy. How are you?"

I didn't really want to go there yet. "First, you tell me how things are going there."

"I've got the beans ready to ship," he said. "It took awhile, but I finally got hold of them."

Excitement bubbled up in my chest. That meant he'd apprehended the guy he was looking for. It couldn't be long until he flew home. "I'm so glad to hear that. And things are...okay here. We had a slow day thanks to the rain."

"How's Kylie doing?" he asked. "She's out of jail now, right?"

Wait a second. I hadn't told him about her getting taken into custody. "How'd you know that?" I asked.

"I asked Detective Hatcher to keep me in the loop, and he did. He also asked me about the vial of GHB and how someone would get their hands on it. I was able to put him in touch with one of my contacts in West Virginia."

A thought occurred to me. "Bo, you didn't—did you spring Kylie from jail?"

He chuckled. "Well, of course I did. That judge set bail higher than anything Kylie could hope to afford, and her parents would never step in on her behalf. Shoot, they'd probably be happy to get Kylie out of the picture so Chelsea would turn tail and head home to them. You know my early retirement from Coffee Mass was a lucrative move, so I was more than happy to get my best barista out of jail and back to work. The Barks & Beans Cafe must go on!"

I laughed, then updated Bo on the everyday things, like Stormy's relatively good behavior and Waffles' adoption by my neighbor. Bo got a kick out of that, saying, "I hope Vera can give that crazy dog a *fur*ever home, as they say."

"Me, too." Getting serious, I said, "Bo, please be careful. And let me know the minute you're back in the country."

"I will. It won't be long now. Thanks for keeping an eye out for Kylie and Chelsea on your end. That puts my mind at ease. Love you, sis."

"I love you, too."

I headed through the connector door into my section of the house, where Coal was once again waiting for me, his loyal tail thumping in my honor. There really was no better morale boost at the end of a long day than coming home to a canine who seemed to think that the sun rose and set with you.

I leaned down to hug him. "Things just keep getting stranger," I murmured into his glossy black fur. "Three people are dead now, and two of them were definitely murdered. I know Kylie didn't do it, but I can't figure out who would've had a good motive. Not that it's my job, but I know this town, and people are going to look at Kylie weird until they see proof she's not a murderer."

Coal whined and tried to snuggle closer to me, which was awkward with his unwieldy body. He wound up half-sitting on my knee.

Stormy waltzed up the hallway. She took in the sight of us, hesitating like she was unsure how she fit into this picture.

I extended a hand, giving a light snap. "Come here, sweetie. Here, kitty, kitty, kitty."

Stormy continued her proud jaunt straight into the bathroom, where she began furiously scratching in the litter box.

I laughed. "I can see how you feel about us, then. Well, your daddy says hello. He's coming back soon." I stood, forcing Coal to back up. After walking down to the kitchen, I rummaged in the fridge to see if I could find anything that struck my fancy for supper. Some of Chelsea's delicious pasta sauce still sat in a container, so I'd just cook some of my frozen tortellini to go with it.

As I went upstairs to change, I reflected on what Bo had told me. *He'd* been the one to pay Kylie's bail, not Nels Hartmann, like I'd assumed. Of course, Nels had covered the lawyer fees, which cost plenty, I was sure. Hopefully that would be the end of the legal bills for Kylie.

Bo had also mentioned that Kylie's parents would probably be glad if she ended up in jail, so Chelsea would come home to them. I couldn't understand why they were so keen to get their youngest home with no regard for their oldest, who was toiling away just to keep her and her sister afloat. While I doubted that the Baers would be capable of murdering people just to get their prodigal daughter back, I wished I could understand them a little better. Why did they seem to hold such a grudge against Kylie for simply trying to spread her wings?

I thought back to what Kylie's dad had said, about her treating him bad after all he'd done for her. Even Kylie had no idea what he was talking about.

Maybe it was time to pay a little visit to the Baers and try to get to the bottom of their dismissive behavior toward Kylie. Even though I doubted I'd get any leads on the murders, at least I could put together a better picture of the kind of environment my barista came from.

But how would I find their address? I could ask Kylie, but she'd demand to know what I was up to. Chelsea wouldn't be as suspicious—in fact, she probably wouldn't even care—so I decided to text her. I'd plugged her cell number into my phone back when she was staying with me.

I changed into my dad's shirt and some looser jeans and

sent her a message, hoping Kylie didn't see it pop up on her sister's phone screen. It only took a minute for her to text back with her parents' address, no questions asked.

Since it wasn't too far from me, I could just dart over to talk to them, then come home and whip up my easy pasta supper. After letting Coal out and putting him in again, I went to my SUV and pulled out. As I made the turn at the end of the street, I heard an engine rev, and a vehicle pulled out behind me. Adjusting my rearview mirror, I was startled to see that the vehicle was a black Jeep Wrangler.

I pounded a fist on my steering wheel. This was getting ridiculous. Jake still hadn't gone home, and now he'd taken to following me around like a regular stalker. I hit the gas, making a quick turn onto a side street before he could catch up to me. If he wanted to talk to me, he could text. This cat-and-mouse game with my ex was really wearing thin.

19

Feeling rattled, I forced myself to slow down and take the back roads to the Baers' house. By the time I pulled into their trailer park on the outskirts of town, there were no vehicles behind me. I tried to shake off my irritation toward Jake and focus on what I'd come here to do—gather information.

The park was a tidy, well-managed place. There were plenty of rocking chairs sitting out on porches, reminding me of all the chats Auntie A and I had shared on ours. I looked forward to early summer, when I could lounge on my porch with nothing better to do than sit and watch the flowers grow, as Auntie A said.

Unlike Bo, I had the capacity to relax for extended periods of time. His idea of unwinding was taking a long jog or shooting at the range. We'd always recharged in completely different ways, but we recognized our differences and tried to be considerate of each other. For instance, Bo had fixed up my porch so it was a cozier place to sit, and I often joined him at the range. Jogging was a real stretch for me, though, so I was glad to leave him to it.

The rain had finally stopped when I walked up the steps to number 23 and knocked on the door. A woman with bottle-blonde hair and saggy skin opened it. "Yeah?"

I realized too late that I hadn't even rehearsed what I was going to say. Maybe it wasn't wise to give her my actual name.

"Uh, hi. I'm a friend of your daughter's, and I wondered if I could ask you a few questions?"

"Which daughter?" she asked, her tone suspicious.

"Both of them," I said.

She looked me up and down with a critical eye. "Have a seat," she said finally, motioning toward a canvas folding chair. Thankfully, it looked like the awning had protected it from the rainstorm, so I sat down. Mrs. Baer sat across from me.

I decided to kick things off in a roundabout way. "Ma'am, I wondered if you'd talked with Emmy Rucker anytime recently?"

Frowning, she said, "Who'd you say you were again? Some kinda cop?"

Hedging around wasn't going to get me anywhere with Mrs. Baer. "No. Actually, your daughter works for me. I'm concerned about her."

She sat back in her chair with a huff. "You're talkin' about Kylie, then."

I nodded. "It seems to me like someone's trying to frame her, so I'm looking into who might want to do that."

"Well, it ain't Emmy Rucker, if you're wonderin' about her. She wouldn't hurt a fly. Now if *I'd* been the one married to Doug Rucker, he'd have been dead years ago. He was a scumbag."

"But I got the impression he was a family friend," I said.

"Maybe a long time ago. When Kylie got hauled in for trying to burn his house down, she wouldn't explain it to me. So I hunted around until I found her diary, and that's when I read what Doug did to her. I tried talking to her, but instead she just up and moved out on her own. Her daddy was going crazy trying to understand why, so I finally told him what I'd read." She shifted in her seat. "Neither one of us was real sober back at that time, mind you. So one night my Tommy got drunk and went over to Doug's and beat the living daylights out of him. That little move got him fired, since they worked together."

Nels Hartmann had only mentioned Mr. Baer's alcoholism as his motivation for firing him. Although that had certainly played a role in things, I wish someone would've told Kylie that her dad had gone out and tried to avenge her, even losing his job in the process.

Mrs. Baer sniffed. "Kylie wouldn't have naught to do with us once she moved out. She won't hear a word edgewise on anything. At least Chelsea will pick up my calls."

"And did you say the two of you are sober now?" I asked.

She hemmed and hawed. "Well, *sober* might be stretching things a little. We both like a little drink here and there, nothing too much, mind you."

I was beginning to get a better picture of why Chelsea clung to her relationship with Kylie. Although Mr. and Mrs. Baer had actually felt a normal level of parental concern for Kylie, their alcoholism was probably an issue that was too big for Kylie to contend with while facing her own pain. It was easier to get out of the house...and eventually to get her sister out, too.

It was still a sad situation, but I felt more hopeful about it. No wonder Mr. Baer had mentioned that he sacrificed for Kylie. He wasn't talking about money—he was talking about losing his job.

"Thank you for answering my questions," I said. "I won't keep you."

"Speaking of Emmy, have you talked to her lately?" Mrs. Baer asked. "I haven't heard from her since the day Doug died. I've been meaning to take her some meatloaf and mashed potatoes."

Of course she didn't know about Emmy's sudden death yet, since Kylie didn't stay in contact with her. I should've thought of that. I was glad she was sitting down.

"I hate to bring bad news, but part of the reason I came is that Emmy Rucker passed away today. She was in a bad car wreck. I guess her car must have skidded into a tree in all that rain."

Her eyes widened. "Emmy? But she always did drive at a snail's pace! Why would she have skidded out?"

"I don't know." Once again, I had the strong impression that Emmy's wreck wasn't an accident. I handed Mrs. Baer a Barks & Beans Cafe business card. "If you think of anyone at all who might have some kind of grudge against Kylie, please let me know."

She stood, her watery blue eyes meeting mine. "Okay. I want to thank you for looking out for Kylie. I do plan to visit your cafe someday...only I'm not sure if Kylie would want me to."

I gave her a noncommittal half-smile. Maybe I could talk to Kylie about that possibility. It seemed like her parents really wanted to mend their relationship with her, and the cafe might be a good place to start, since it was neutral ground.

As I stepped off the porch, Mrs. Baer called after me. "Oh, yeah, some guy named Corey did come over last week, sniffing around for Chelsea. Said she had something that belonged to him. Tommy shooed him off right quick, though. He said the kid looked like he was high. I don't know if that would have anything to do with Kylie, though."

"Okay, thanks for telling me," I said. As I got into my SUV, I tried to fit the pieces together. Corey wanted Alec's drugs—that much was clear. Had he killed Alec, thinking he could swoop in and take over his drug racket? Also, why was he so convinced that Chelsea had the stash? Was she lying to everyone?

And where did Doug and Emmy Rucker come into the equation? If this were a TV show, they might be cast as the everyday couple that were operating a drug ring from their home. Yet that didn't seem to fit. Emmy didn't like Doug, so she wouldn't be working with him. And the police had probably searched her house after Doug's murder, so I couldn't imagine she would've been hiding a major drug cache there.

There had to be a connection between the two—and now possibly three—victims. As I drove along the gravel roundabout that connected the trailers, I had to admit that the only connection I could see was Kylie. She knew every one of the victims, and someone was trying really hard to make it look like she was a killer.

I sighed. I had tracked down everyone suspicious I could find, and I was still no closer to figuring out who framed Kylie. As I neared my street, I felt a sense of irritation. If

Jake's Jeep was parked there, I'd walk straight over and give him a piece of my mind. If he'd been harboring even *one* single hope of getting back with me—which was foolish in the first place—he would've blown it to smithereens by his stalker behavior. I was at the point where I simply wanted him out of my life.

Then again, my resolve always weakened the moment Jake walked up in the flesh. It was easy to rehash his failings when he was gone, but it was another thing altogether to hold onto that pain when he was standing right next to me, his familiar voice and smell and lips pulling me in like a bug to a Venus flytrap.

The coast was clear as I pulled up to the curb. Although it was getting dusky, Vera was walking down the sidewalk toward me with Waffles on a leash by her side.

She beamed at me and asked, "How are you, Macy?"

I gave Waffles a scratch behind the ear. "I should ask how are *you*? Is Waffles learning the ropes?"

She grinned. "We did have quite the night as she got used to her new crate. But today she's started going into it on her own, so I think that's a good sign."

"She didn't have any accidents?" I asked.

"Not a one." Vera looked at her new dog proudly. "And she's very obedient."

I never would have guessed I'd hear anyone say those words in regard to Waffles. I squatted in front of the pretty Labradoodle, trying to read the emotions in her little dark eyes. She cocked her head at me before launching into a scratching frenzy on her right side.

"She's been treated for fleas," Vera reassured me. "I think she might have some dry skin."

Something told me that Vera was going to be able to give

Waffles all the attention she needed. She'd found her companion dog, and I was pleased as punch to see it.

"You'll have to bring her over to meet Coal sometime," I offered, then immediately regretted it. Although Waffles was used to being around other dogs in the shelter, I wasn't sure how she would do one-on-one.

"I'd love to," Vera said. "Let's set something up. But right now, I'm taking her in for a little treat since she did so great on her walk."

Waffles' silky ears perked up when she heard the magic word *treat*. She stood to attention at Vera's side.

I grinned. "I'm so happy for both of you."

Vera gave me a quick hug. "And I have you to thank for it! I've been telling all my friends about the Barks & Beans Cafe."

I only hoped her glowing recommendation didn't dim over time.

AFTER EATING MY PASTA, I decided that I needed to put the kibosh on Jake's lurking. I let Coal sit on the couch next to me while I made the call. Jake picked up on the first ring.

"Macy, how are you?" he asked.

I didn't beat around the bush. "Jake, why have you been following me around? I saw you on my road today."

"I was trying to catch up to you. You won't answer my texts."

"Have you ever stopped to think there might be a reason for that? Jake, I appreciate that you came up to join us for the cafe's anniversary, but now it's really time for you to go home.

Bo's coming back soon, and we'll have a lot to catch up on when he gets here."

Jake fell silent, probably pondering the implications of what I'd just said. Bo was coming home, and he hadn't seen Jake since he walked out on me. Jake had to understand that Bo would not look on his visit kindly.

"Oh, okay. I understand." His voice had lost some of its usual confidence. "Well, Dad wanted me to get back, anyway. Could we get together one more time before I leave, do you think? I brought something that I wanted to show you."

"Why don't you just tell me what it is?" I said, my frustration building. He'd moved out of our rental house long before I did, so I knew he hadn't found anything of mine lying around.

Then the thought occurred to me that he might have *bought* me something, like jewelry, in an attempt to make up. If that were the case, he had to be delusional. What did he think I was going to do—remarry him and let him move in with Coal and me?

"I want to show you in person," he insisted. "I swear, I'll get out of your hair after that."

Out of my hair did sound promising. "Okay," I finally agreed. "We can meet in the cafe."

"I can't come tomorrow since I have to do several online training sessions, but how about Wednesday?" he asked.

"Sure. Just swing by around noon, when I take my lunch break."

I hung up, feeling somewhat better. Although I couldn't guess what Jake had up his sleeve, he had basically promised to leave after our meeting. Then I could pull my focus back to the cafe, where it should've been all along.

20

I WATCHED the sunrise from the cafe on Tuesday morning, enjoying how the pink and gold streaks eased into a beautiful shade of robin's egg blue. My spirits lifted to see that the weather was looking good, so we'd definitely have more customers.

Summer dropped off three dogs, each one adorable. As we were chatting, Kylie walked over to tell me that she'd decided to let Chelsea return to her job today. "We can't live in fear," she said. "I gave her a pepper spray, since she's not too handy with a knife."

While I worried about both women being out where Corey could find them, I offered Kylie an encouraging smile. "She'll be fine. As Bo always says, 'To be forewarned is to be forearmed.'"

Kylie grinned. I felt the urge to share about my visit with her mom, but that would best be done in private.

As Kylie headed back to the coffee bar, Summer raised her eyebrows at me. "What's up with Miss Congeniality?"

she whispered. "I've never seen her act like that before. It's almost like she trusts you or something."

"I guess maybe she does," I admitted. "I tried to be there for her—"

"Of course you did," Summer finished. An excited look crossed her face and she extended her hand, frantically patting at my arm. "Hey, I have a great idea. Kylie and her sister have been under a lot of stress lately, right? What if we all got together for a girls' night? I could bring my buffalo chicken dip and you could get the veggies and nachos. Then we could make brownies together and—"

"Hang on," I said, shooting another look toward Kylie. "I don't know if she's the girls' night type."

Summer threw her hands up. "Pshaw," she said. "Every girl needs time to unwind every now and again, even that one. Trust me. I can *sense* that she's ready for friendship."

A slow smile spread across my face. Kylie and Chelsea had probably felt alone against the world for many years, so I liked the idea of showing them things didn't have to be that way. "Okay, I'm game. Do you want to invite her or should I?"

Summer leaned down, giving the dogs some final pets. "You do it. I'm still a little afraid of her. Just let me know what time you all decide on and I'll be there with the dip." She turned and flitted through the dog gate, her long skirt swishing.

I headed over to the coffee bar. Jimmy grinned at me and continued his morning prep work. Taking Kylie aside, I asked if she'd want to come over tonight, and to my surprise, she readily agreed.

"I'll bring my caramel brownie mix," she offered. "And I can whip us up some iced decaf drinks, too."

As I headed back to the dog section, I texted Summer that Kylie and Chelsea would come over at six.

"I knew it," she texted back. "I'll be there with enough dip to drown in."

Six o'clock rolled around faster than I thought. Since Coal already knew everyone coming, I didn't worry about putting him upstairs, which is what I usually did when our Sunday school class came over.

The house was tidied and all the veggies were chopped when Kylie and Chelsea arrived. Coal hurtled straight toward Kylie, and Stormy darted toward Chelsea. As they were loving on the pets, Summer showed up with a huge Crockpot full of dip. "Let's get this party started!" she shouted.

Any thoughts of Kylie's former standoffishness and Chelsea's sullen behavior floated into the wind. Tonight, we were going to bond over food and pets and good conversation. Summer must've sensed I needed this night, too, because I was already starting to feel relaxed.

After stuffing ourselves, we lounged on the couch for awhile, talking. Chelsea had us all rolling after sharing several incidents she'd seen at House of Burgers, and Summer launched into some select tales from the shelter. Coal sat on his pillow, a contented look on his face. Stormy behaved like a jungle cat, letting out loud meows every now and then while roaming along the back of the couch.

Summer suggested we start mixing the brownies, so I followed her into the kitchen and gathered what we needed to bake them. Kylie pulled a bag of coffee beans from her tote and started grinding coffee for decaf lattes.

A brief guitar tune sounded from Chelsea's phone. As she glanced at it, she briefly drew her eyebrows together. "I should probably take that," she said. "I have a friend at work who's having issues." Turning to me, she asked, "Would you mind if I went back into your guest room and talked to her? It might take awhile." Her tone was apologetic.

"Oh, sure, no worries," I said. Chelsea had certainly come a long way in a short period of time. Not only was she more engaged in life now, but she was also reaching out to friends in need. It warmed my heart to watch her transformation.

THE ENTIRE HOUSE smelled like caramel brownies and coffee, which was my idea of paradise. We settled into our chairs, ready to dig in.

Kylie leaned in and whispered, "How long's she been in there?"

"I don't know," Summer said. "I think it's been at least thirty-five minutes, given how long those brownies took to bake."

Kylie placed a finger to her lips and tiptoed down the hallway. She tilted toward the guest room door, listening. After a couple of minutes, she gave a knock and said, "Brownies are ready!"

We didn't hear a response, and apparently Kylie didn't, either, since she turned the knob. It was locked. She shot me a concerned look. "Can you open this?"

I scrambled to my feet. "Sure. All I have to do is get a toothpick and stick it in that little hole." I grabbed one and popped the lock.

As I pushed the door open, it was immediately evident that Chelsea wasn't in the room. Although she'd left a light on, the side window was cracked just enough to let her slip out.

"She ran off." Kylie's voice was filled with dismay. "Why would she even *do* that? She seemed to have quit all her old ways after Alec died."

I didn't want to consider it, but maybe Chelsea was the connecting puzzle piece, the person who seemed to be lurking in the background all this time. Like Kylie, she, too, knew all the people who'd been murdered. She'd been directly involved with a drug dealer, and his right-hand man was looking for her, convinced she'd hidden the drug supply somewhere.

Then again, maybe Corey had somehow snatched her from my house...but Coal definitely would have heard and barked if someone had crept up to the window.

Kylie's wild eyes told me her thoughts were running along the same lines.

Summer stepped into the room behind us and guessed what had happened. "Uh, oh," she said. "What do we do now?"

"I don't want to call the police yet," Kylie said. "It seems like she ran off on her own, wouldn't you say?"

"I agree," I said. "Chelsea would have screamed if Corey broke in, and he would've had to shatter the glass, since he couldn't have opened the locked window from the outside. Anyway, Coal would've alerted us to any sounds of a scuffle."

"I agree," Kylie said. "But she didn't even have a vehicle. My keys were in the living room with us."

"Does she know how to hotwire?" Summer asked.

Kylie's look darkened. "I honestly couldn't say. Maybe I don't know my sister as well as I thought. I'll go check." She raced into the living room and out the back door.

Coal trotted up behind me, his look anxious. "It'll be okay, boy," I said, stroking his ear and hoping I was right. Maybe Chelsea had walked off to meet her work friend. But it was dark out, so that was a pretty strange move.

"Maybe her friend was a guy," Summer suggested. "Maybe he wasn't a great guy, and she didn't want Kylie to know about him?"

"Possibly." I glanced around, searching for any clues as to Chelsea's whereabouts, but nothing was amiss.

Kylie returned. "My car's still there," she said. "She must've gone somewhere on foot."

"Do you know which friend she was talking to?" I asked. "Or was that a cover story, do you think?"

"I don't have any idea." She snapped her fingers. "Wait—I almost forgot. I set up a family finder app on her phone about a month ago. I haven't even used it yet. Let me see if it works."

She clicked on the app and typed something in. In just a moment, she turned the phone toward us, a pinpointed location highlighted on a map.

"She's in Lewisburg," she said triumphantly. Touching the screen to make the map bigger, she said, "She's over on Rhododendron Drive. Have either of you been there?"

Summer nodded. "It's that ritzy part of town up on the hill. Gated drives, big houses, and all that."

Kylie frowned. "What on earth would she be doing

there?"

"We can take my car," I offered. "Let's check it out. At least we know right where she is."

I clipped my knife into my pocket and Summer noticed. "Do you think we should call the cops?" she whispered.

Kylie overheard her. "No cops, at least not yet. Just let me grab something from my car." She headed into the darkness, returning a few minutes later with a long, sheathed knife I was betting she kept tucked under a seat. "I doubt Chelsea's into any trouble in that neighborhood. There's probably a good explanation for this. But just in case, we'll be ready." She shoved the knife sheath into the side of her jeans and pulled her leather jacket over top of it. "Let's go."

As I drove over, I wondered if we were possibly being hypervigilant. Maybe this was what parents of rebellious teens felt like every single day. It would be exhausting.

"She's probably gone over to talk with her friend, who happens to live in a nice neighborhood," Kylie said, more to herself than to us. "But I tried calling and texting her and didn't get any answers, so that's strange."

Rhododendron Drive proved to be a long loop, with about six huge homes situated down tree-lined drives. A couple of the houses had gates in front, including the one we were heading toward.

I pulled to a stop off to the side of the driveway. "You sure this is the right place?" I asked.

Kylie stared at her phone. "Yes, it's saying it's number 233."

We peered up the drive. Quite a few lights were blazing in the house. "It looks on the up and up," I remarked.

"Yeah," Kylie said. "I've got to go up there and check on her. I'll head in myself."

I grabbed her arm. "No way. I'm going with you."

Summer piped up from the back seat. "Me, too."

I turned. "No, I think it's best if one of us stays here, just in case." I pulled up Detective Hatcher's cell number and wrote it down for Summer. "If we don't come back in about fifteen minutes or so—actually, make it twenty in case we find out we know these people and get to talking—then call the detective and tell him what's going on."

Summer grabbed the paper and nodded. "Okay."

"I don't think we'll have any issues—after all, we're two armed women, right? It's not like we're going into this blind," I added.

Summer looked dubious as Kylie opened her door. "Still, you never know. Be careful."

I got out, coming around to stand next to Kylie as she examined the closed gate. There was a button built into the brick pillar beside it. "Should we buzz in?" I asked. "That would be the easiest way."

Kylie considered it a moment. "I'd feel better about it if I knew who lived here, and my phone isn't telling me that information." She strode over and examined the shrub-lined fence, walking down the road a little way. As she rounded the fence corner, she gave a short whistle.

I jogged over. "What is it?" I asked.

She held a shrub to the side. "A hidden gate," she said. "I tried it, and it's unlocked."

This was starting to feel all wrong. "What if they have attack dogs?" I asked.

Kylie already had the gate open and was heading in. "You're good with dogs."

I crept in behind her, pulling the gate closed behind us. "That is *not* the right answer."

21

Kylie moved like a ninja along the edge of the darkened driveway. I lost sight of her several times since her dark hair and clothing acted like camouflage.

As she drew closer to the circle of light near the house, she turned and whispered, "You coming?"

I dashed over to her side. "I'm here. Now what? Do we go up and ring the doorbell? They might not be too happy we bypassed the gate, no matter how nice a family they happen to be."

She cocked her head, listening. "At least they don't seem to have any dogs. How about this—I'll skirt around the place and look in the windows. Surely with all those lights on, I'll catch a glimpse of Chelsea."

I peered up at the looming brick house. "But it's two stories. What if she's upstairs somewhere?"

"We'll rework the plan as needed," she said firmly, as if she'd been in charge of a thousand secret operations before.

She darted off toward the side of the house. I held my breath as she popped up under one window, then another. I couldn't hear any noise coming from inside, which was strange with all those lights burning, but I supposed that since this was a newer build, the house would be well-insulated and pretty soundproof.

It didn't take her long to return. "I didn't see anyone, and I'm tired of waiting around. I called her again and she didn't answer. I'm ringing the doorbell." She pulled her knife from its sheath, gripping it behind her back with one hand. She marched up to the front porch and pushed the lit button. I could see the knife blade glinting.

Kylie reminded me so much of Bo, who also refused to consult anyone before charging into trouble. Still, I wish she'd given me a chance to prepare. I hustled up to her side just as the wide wooden door opened.

I couldn't place the familiar-looking, casually dressed older man who stood in the doorway. "Kylie?" he asked.

She looked confused. "Mr. Hartmann?"

Nels Hartmann gave her an understanding look. "I guess you're here looking for Chelsea. She came over awhile ago— she's still here."

Kylie's knife sagged. "But why?"

I was trying to work that out myself. Was Chelsea seeing the older man? Was he the "friend" she'd lied to us about? I supposed he was handsome in his own way, and as far as I knew, still a widower. But there was quite an extreme age gap between them. If Chelsea was with Nels, no wonder she'd been reluctant to tell Kylie the truth.

"Come in, please," he said, ushering us inside. "I'm not sure if Detective Hatcher called you yet, but there's been another tragedy. I went ahead and let Chelsea know, since my lawyer—he's actually the lawyer who helped you out,

Kylie—needed to ask her a few questions about it. They're in the other room, just through the foyer."

I followed Kylie into the rounded entryway, which was lined with paintings and marble statues. With a crystal-encrusted French chandelier sparkling overhead, the space truly warranted the formal-sounding title of "foyer," which I'd only heard used in reference to a church entryway. Kylie covertly shifted her knife back into its sheath, probably breathing a sigh of relief that there was a reasonable explanation for Chelsea's sudden disappearance.

It did concern me that the lawyer had asked to talk with Chelsea and not Kylie in relation to whatever fresh tragedy had occurred. Did that mean that Chelsea was more closely associated with the situation, or that Kylie was going to be a lead suspect yet again?

A dark-stained spiral staircase wound off to the left, and a pale blue dining room opened up on the right. Nels continued straight on through a double French door that opened into a large, window-lined sitting area. Pale velvet couches were situated in groupings around an indoor water fountain. The sound of flowing water enhanced the relaxing feel of the room.

Glancing around, he said, "They must've headed into the living room. I'll show you in there."

He led us through a closed door that gave onto a tight, darkly-lit bar room. The house's floor plan wasn't the least bit instinctive, and it was beginning to feel like a labyrinth. I found myself wondering where the kitchen was located, or if Nels even had a kitchen at all. Given the size of his house, I supposed he could eat out every night if he wanted. When people in town called him a paving "magnate," they weren't exaggerating.

Kylie finally spoke up. "What kind of tragedy were you talking about? Why did Chelsea need to talk to your lawyer? How did she get over here?"

Nels stopped short as he turned to face us in the confined space. "I'm sure my lawyer will explain everything, but unfortunately, this evening, Corey was found dead in an old house where drug users tend to congregate. Somebody freaked out when they saw his body and left an anonymous tip with the cops about where he was at." He pushed a door open, gesturing with a wide flourish to Kylie. "Ladies first," he said, offering a polite smile.

I'd fallen behind, but as I hurried to catch up, Nels stepped directly behind Kylie as she crossed the threshold of the door.

And then, to my horror, he placed a firm hand on her back, giving her a tremendous shove. I heard the terrible sounds of her body as it thudded down stairs she hadn't anticipated. Her immediate cries of pain told me she'd been injured, possibly badly.

I rushed at Nels, but he'd already slammed the door shut and whipped back toward me.

"Get her," he bellowed. Powerful arms grabbed me from behind, wrapping me up like a fish in a net. I couldn't see who my captor was.

"What are you *doing*?" I shouted. "Kylie! Are you okay?"

I heard a small, mumbled response, and then Nels barked out further instructions to his henchman. "Walk this one down, too, and be sure to get the brunette's phone." He stepped closer to me. "But first, I'll need to take a couple of things." He delicately slid his hand into my front jeans pocket, extracting my knife. "I thought that's what that metal clip was," he said, grinning. "And where have you hidden your phone, Macy?"

I cringed at the thought of him touching me again, so I made it easy on him. "In my back pocket," I said.

The man behind me grabbed it. My captor's beefy hand engulfed my phone as he thrust it toward Nels, and his hot breath hit my hair from such a high angle, I could tell he was huge. Struggling against him would definitely be pointless.

"Thanks for your cooperation." Nels smirked. "And now for a few house rules. We'll have no funny business or escape attempts. I hadn't planned on all three of you, but the more the merrier, right?"

Kylie moaned from downstairs. "She's hurt," I said. "You have to help her."

"Oh, I will. We'll make sure you're all in tip-top shape before we ship you out."

"Ship us out?"

Nels cocked his head toward the basement door, and my captor steered me toward it. I dug my feet in and struggled against him, unwilling to get shoved downstairs.

But instead of pushing me, the man simply picked me up like a sack of potatoes and slung me over his shoulder.

"Put those two in with the other," Nels ordered. "I'll talk with Leo first, but he'll probably want all three. And don't you dare touch the goods."

My stomach clenched when he said that name. There was only one Leo involved in the criminal underworld in our area, and that was Leo Moreau.

And Leo had plenty of reasons to want Bo Hatfield's sister dead.

The henchman grunted and carried me downstairs. Kylie was lying on the stair landing, her lips twisted in pain as she cradled one of her elbows. When she saw me, she tried to scramble to her feet, but my captor simply yanked her up by her jacket as he walked by.

She cried out in pain, but he ignored her. After roughly setting me down, he dragged us both over toward a darkened far corner of the basement and flipped on a light. I couldn't believe what I saw.

Just in front of us was a metal-barred holding area, very similar to a prison cell. And inside, lying silent on a flimsy mattress, was Chelsea.

Kylie's screams turned hysterical. "What'd you *do* to her? Is she dead?" She clawed at the man's viselike hand, trying to escape. I struggled against him, too, pulling in the opposite direction. But it was useless. He pinned Kylie under his huge arm so he could unlock the cell, then wordlessly shoved us both in.

"Give me your phone," he ordered Kylie.

After haltingly extracting the phone from her jacket pocket with her good arm, Kylie shoved it through the bars. The man wrapped it in his fingers and locked the door. He hit the light again, throwing us into partial darkness. Kylie stumbled over toward Chelsea.

"She's breathing." Kylie's voice was shaky.

"Thank goodness," I said. "But what about you? What happened?"

"I fell all the way down those stairs, but thankfully I didn't fall off the side. It's a sheer drop onto the concrete floor. I think I might've broken my elbow when I hit the landing, since I heard it pop. And my arm feels numb—I can't bring it up. When I move it the wrong way, pain rips through it."

I wished I knew some kind of emergency medical

technique to help, but a broken elbow was nothing like the dislocated shoulders they always showed on TV, where all you had to do was pop things back into place.

"You should lie down," I said. "You've been through a shock."

The other section of the basement fell dark as the man turned off the lights. I let my eyes adjust, but there wasn't a sliver of light visible anywhere...which would indicate that there weren't any windows.

"You've been through a shock too!" Kylie said. I could hear the anger working its way up through her pain. "What is Nels even *doing*? He can't think he'll get away with kidnapping all three of us. What on earth is his plan here?"

"He said something about getting us in good shape before he shipped us out." I didn't mention Leo, but the fact that he was involved told me that this wasn't some small-town operation. "I'm guessing human trafficking."

"You're kidding me," she said. "Does this tie in with Alec and Doug's murders, do you think? Were they involved with Nels' schemes?"

"I have no idea."

Chelsea groaned. Kylie began murmuring to her sister, urging her to wake up.

I felt around at the cell bars, finally locating the padlock. "You still have your knife, right?" I whispered.

"I do," Kylie said. It took a couple of moments, but she made her way over to me. "Good thing it was in its sheath and not in my hand when I fell down those stairs. I probably would've stabbed myself to death."

I cringed to think of how much worse things could've been. "Very true. Here, I'm stretching out my hands. Just set the knife in them, then you can go sit with Chelsea."

Kylie did as I asked. I felt the cold blade against my palms. Wrapping my hands around the wooden handle, I pointed the sharp business end toward the padlock and tried to work the point into the keyhole.

"He's...crazy," Chelsea said quietly.

It was a relief to hear her say something coherent.

Kylie said, "We figured that out. But what happened to you?"

"He texted me that Corey had been found dead. He said that although it looked like a drug overdose, one of your knives was stuck in him. He said the lawyer needed to talk to me and get all the details of my story right before the police came knocking on your door, which they inevitably would. He sent his car over to pick me up over on Main Street."

Kylie sounded livid. "And you snuck out and took off with him without telling me a thing?"

Now Chelsea's voice filled with irritation. "I was worried about you, sis. I didn't want another murder getting pinned on you."

"He didn't mention Kylie's knife when he told us about Corey," I said, giving a careful twist of the blade tip in the lock. I hope it didn't mess up the keyhole somehow.

"It could all be a pack of lies, for all we know," Kylie said darkly. "It seems like his main objective was to get Chelsea."

An overhead light suddenly flipped on. As someone walked down the steps, I realized that the tail end of our conversation might have been overheard. Nels Hartmann came into view, walking straight toward us.

I quickly but carefully slid the sheathless knife into the back of my waistband, hoping I didn't stab myself in the process. Leaning against the bars, I shouted, "Let us out!" Hopefully, Nels hadn't caught sight of what I was doing.

Maybe if he came close enough, I could grab his shirt and stab him...but then how would we get the cell unlocked? Besides, I was terrible with the sight of blood. If I did manage to work up the courage to stab him, I'd likely pass out in the process. I threw a desperate look at Kylie, wishing she were next to me. I had no doubt she'd have the guts to knife the man who'd kidnapped her sister.

A glimmer of hope shot through me as I recalled that Summer was waiting outside. Surely twenty minutes had passed since the time we'd crept toward the house. She must have called Detective Hatcher in by now.

Unless she'd decided to come in and get us herself...but surely she wouldn't have done something so foolhardy. Maybe we just had to keep this guy talking until the detective and his men could surround the place.

Nels' confident smile seemed to mock us. "Well, ladies, how are we doing?"

Kylie slowly rose from the bed and walked over to my side. She placed a hand on my back as if she were too weak to stand on her own, but I felt her gingerly working the knife up out of my jeans.

"You broke my elbow, you freak," she snapped.

Nels smiled wider. "You always were the feisty one—I remember how you tried to torch Doug Rucker, way back when. I couldn't take any chances with you."

"You knew about that?" she asked. I couldn't feel the blade against my back, so I had to believe Kylie was now gripping the knife in her good hand.

"Of course. I make it a point to know about my employees' lives. It was a shame I had to fire your dad for beating Doug up, but Doug was more valuable to me, you see."

Kylie looked confused. "But Dad said it was the alcohol—"

"I gave him a good severance pay if he agreed to stick to the cover story," Nels said. "I couldn't let it get out what kind of a man Doug was, otherwise my other employees would've asked too many questions about why I kept him on. But you just wouldn't let things go, would you?" He leaned closer to her. "In fact, you've been a thorn in my side ever since I've known you, Kylie Baer." Throwing a softer glance over Kylie's shoulder at Chelsea, he continued. "For a long time, you've been standing in the way of what I want. Your sister is perfection, with her classical beauty and all that fair hair. She'll fetch a pretty penny in my circles. But every time I tried to get close—at office picnics or wherever—you'd step in and get her away from me." He frowned. "It was almost like you could tell what I was doing. Then you went a step further and moved her in with you, so I didn't have any believable reason to see her anymore."

Kylie hauled off and spat in his face. "Guess I must've picked up on what a slimy old pervert you are."

The man took out a tissue and slowly wiped off the spit that dribbled off his chin. "But, my dear, you have no recourse. It seems you've murdered...hm...four people now, is it? Alec, Doug, Emmy, and now poor Corey. Why, you should thank me for sending you off to a country where you'll never come up for trial."

"You'll never get away with this." Kylie's voice was determined, and I sensed she was about to make her move.

"On the contrary." Before either of us had a chance to realize what he was doing, Nels extended a hand and plunged a hypodermic needle into Kylie's bad arm. She started to scream, but soon dropped to the floor in a heap. Her long knife clattered to the floor beside her.

I quickly backed out of Nels' reach, horrified at the turn things had taken.

Chelsea pulled herself out of bed and crawled over to her sister's side. "Kylie, Kylie," she wailed, holding her sister's face in her hands.

He stared at Kylie's impressive weapon on the floor. "I should've known she'd be armed," he said. "After all, I'm familiar with her affinity for blades and swords. I've actually bought several of them through third parties over the years...of course, now those exact weapons been taken into evidence against her." He tilted his chin toward me. "And what about you, Miss Macy? Have you any tricks up your sleeve?"

Furious at how he'd hurt my brave friend, I stared him dead in the eyes. My arms started shaking with anger as I thought of Bo and said, "You might be surprised."

The devious man just laughed. "Don't delude yourself. I know all about your tragic past, Macy Hatfield. Orphaned as a child, you have no parents and no family left, except for a brother who's currently out of town. You're just as vulnerable as these two girls...and you're every bit as marketable with that cloud of red-blonde hair. Lean in a little. What shade of blue are your eyes again? I want to be sure to get my description right."

I considered spitting on him, but I needed to keep my cool. He'd talked about shipping us out, and I needed to make sure that didn't happen before the police showed up. "What did you give her?" I asked, trying to stall as I motioned to Kylie's limp body.

"Same thing she gave her 'victims,'" he said calmly. "It's a little knockout drug called GHB." He leered at me. "You might not know it yet, but they're going to find it in Emmy Rucker's body, too."

"But Emmy wasn't in your network of crime, was she? Who really killed her, and why?" At the very least, I might be able to get a murder confession out of him.

He shot a look at Chelsea, who was still helplessly sitting by her sister's side. "What happened was that Emmy got a little too concerned when the police took Kylie into custody for Doug's murder. I should've known she had a soft spot for the girl. She was on her way to turn herself in when her car so unfortunately ran off the road."

"What do you mean, *turn herself in?*" I asked.

He chuckled. "Oh, but haven't you connected the dots yet? Emmy Rucker drugged and then stabbed her husband, of course."

22

Oh, no. That wasn't what he was supposed to say. "You're lying through your teeth," I said. "Emmy Rucker couldn't have killed Doug. She didn't have it in her."

The twisted smile he gave me was pure evil. "You'd be surprised what people are capable of, especially if you make things easy for them. Emmy didn't know where that knife came from, and I assured her it would never be traced back to her. Of course, I didn't elaborate on the fact that I knew it *would* be traced back to Kylie. I gave Emmy the knockout drug and told her how much to squirt in Doug's afternoon glass of sweet tea. Once he was down, it was simple enough for me to send a car for him. She rode along, stabbed him, then left his body with my guy to deal with, as we'd agreed."

"Your guy? You mean that man who grabbed me?"

He chuckled. "Oh, no. That man is someone Leo sent over to retrieve Chelsea tonight. *My* guy had already killed before, so he was quite amenable to doing what I asked." He gave Chelsea a pitying look. "Young love is so complicated, isn't it? You never would have guessed that I told Alec

Marchand to insinuate his way into your life—and your house. He was winsome, wasn't he, dear girl? And *so* happy to do what I asked so he could keep in his steady supply of drugs, too. Of course, he was the one who hid that GHB in your sister's purse months ago."

Chelsea's pale face reddened in anger. "You're saying you *planted* Alec in my life?"

"I did. And then, when he'd done his job of easing you out of your sister's grip and making you comfortable with sneaking out of the house, I told Corey I could help *him* take over the operation. He was more than happy to jump at the chance to run Alec's lucrative business. After using the knockout drug I supplied, he stabbed Alec with Kylie's sword, taking care to hide the body in the open near her weapons stand. He said he had a close call when Kylie started chasing after him, but later he felt certain she hadn't seen his face."

I recalled the man in the dark hoodie who'd bumped into me at the flea market that day. So that had been Corey, just as Kylie had suspected but hadn't been able to prove.

Chills ran up my spine as it dawned on me that, even though the wealthy man standing in front of me was heartlessly poised to sell us off to the highest bidder, he hadn't yet confessed to killing anyone. He'd simply aided them in doing what they'd already wanted to do, thus advancing his own ends.

He was a master manipulator, a schemer who had decided he was going to get his hands on Chelsea years ago, when she was only a teenager. Then he'd ruthlessly set about his plan to do just that...firing her father, fomenting rebellion against her sister with a conveniently placed boyfriend, setting Kylie up for prison to get her out of the way, and finally—probably when he became desperate—luring Chelsea to his house with the story that she had to talk to his lawyer in order to protect Kylie from the next murder accusation.

Had he ever truly gotten his hands dirty in an actual murder? Something pushed me to find out, even as I felt the time slipping away from me. Why hadn't Detective Hatcher showed up yet?

"So you're saying that you gave Emmy that drug, then ran her car off the road so she couldn't talk to the police?" I asked.

Without answering, he pulled a key from his pocket and inserted it into the lock. A sense of dread washed over me. He opened the door and took a step inside, his eyes locked on Kylie's knife where it lay untouched on the floor. Chelsea was sobbing over her sister as if she had no strength left. I was sure that could be a side effect of the knockout medicine Nels must have given her earlier.

I backed up as he advanced toward me. "No, my dear, I'm *not* saying I gave Emmy that medicine and ran her off the road. By the way, if you think you're gathering evidence on me, you might as well forget it. Where you're going, like I said, no one cares. Let's just say you won't be needing a passport when you travel the way Leo will send you." He gave me a contemplative look. "Then again, Leo was *most* interested when I told him what the cat had dragged into my house tonight. He might want to keep you around. It seems there's some bad blood between him and that big brother of yours."

I took one more step backward and felt the wall behind me. There was nowhere to hide. I was going to have to fight for my freedom—without getting jabbed by the hypodermic needle he was clutching in his fist.

Bo had taught me some basic self-defense moves, but I doubted they'd work in this situation. The moment I tried to punch or kick, Nels would get me with the needle.

Much as I hated to leave Chelsea and Kylie behind, there was no way they were up to an escape. I needed to race for the open door and somehow snap the padlock shut on Nels.

For some reason, a random nature fact sprang to mind. I recalled that you're supposed to run in a zigzag pattern to get away from a bear. Although there wasn't much space between me and the door, it seemed like it might be a halfway decent plan.

I darted left, and when Nels lunged that way, I quickly shifted direction, jumping over Kylie's body and bolting through the door. I fumbled with the lock, but Nels was already racing toward me, so I let the door swing open. "I'll come back!" I shouted at Chelsea, tearing toward the staircase. As I reached the lower landing, I spied a light switch on the wall and hit it, plunging the stairs into quasi-darkness.

Hugging the wall as I went up so I didn't tumble over the open side of the stairs, I finally reached the closed door. After feeling for the knob, I whipped the door open and rushed out. Pulling it shut behind me, I twisted the lock. As I did so, strong arms once again wrapped me from behind.

"No!" I shouted, desperately trying to wriggle away. I was so close to getting out of this house of horrors. "Let me go!"

To my surprise, the arms immediately released and a wonderfully familiar voice sounded above me. "Macy, it's me. Sorry—I didn't want you to fall."

I did a slow turn. Titan McCoy stood there, in all his six-foot-five FBI glory. He was wearing a bulletproof vest and he carried an intimidating pistol on his hip.

His eyes filled with concern. "Summer told us," he said briefly. "Are you okay?"

I nodded, speechless.

"Nels is down there?" he asked, drawing his gun.

"He's right behind me; that's why I locked him in," I managed.

"Okay." He gestured to the side door that led toward the front of the house. "Listen, I need you to go straight through that door, where you'll find an officer waiting. Tell him I want him to walk you out to Detective Hatcher. The rest of the house is already secure—they've already picked up the big guy who was hiding out upstairs. I'm going to retrieve Nels."

I didn't wait around. As I raced straight into the fountain room, I heard the basement door crash open behind me. Titan's voice boomed, "Get on the floor! FBI!"

Once the officer caught sight of me, he took my arm and escorted me toward the front door. My frantic breathing refused to slow, even though my brain registered that I was finally safe.

I wasn't sure how or why Titan had been called in on this job, but one thing I did know—Nels Hartmann's reign of terror was over. I could only hope Leo Moreau would be next.

23

Two officers in vests passed us as we exited the front door. They must be heading in as backup for Titan, although I doubted he needed it. Hopefully, they'd get Kylie and Chelsea out as soon as Nels was in cuffs.

Summer was waiting outside, huddled in a blanket near the back of an ambulance. She ran toward me the minute she saw me, wrapping me in a hug as I stepped off the porch. "You're safe!" Peering behind me, she asked, "But where's Kylie? Did you find Chelsea?"

"Long story," I said wearily.

Detective Hatcher smacked the top of a police cruiser, which pulled out. The burly guy who'd grabbed me sat in the back seat, shooting me a dark glare. Maybe he'd give Moreau up as a human trafficker, but knowing how things usually went for Moreau's henchman, he might wind up dead first.

The detective jogged over to me. "You okay? Summer called and told me what happened. I knew the Bureau had looked into Nels several years back in regard to a girl who went missing in a neighboring county, but they'd never been able to prove anything. The fact that you two went in and didn't come out raised all kinds of red flags, so I got in touch with our friend Titan McCoy."

"I'm sure Bo would appreciate your forethought," I said. "Listen, when they bring Kylie and Chelsea out, they're probably going to need medical attention since Nels injected them with GHB. Also, I think Kylie broke her elbow in a fall."

The detective motioned to a nearby paramedic. After the man asked me if I was okay and I assured him I was, the detective told him what to expect when the women were brought out.

Summer and I moved a little closer to a police car so we'd be out of the way. When I shivered, she wrapped me in her blanket.

"Thank you for calling the detective," I said. "You were literally my only hope. He was going to ship us who knows where, and Kylie and Chelsea weren't with the program."

Summer wrapped an arm around me. "I wasn't about to let you disappear. I had the feeling something was going wrong, so I actually called him a few minutes early."

I got teary-eyed. "You might have saved my life when you did that. I'd hate to think what might have happened if they didn't catch Nels and that brute when they did."

"So *the* Nels Hartmann was behind the recent murders?" she asked, incredulous. "Single and charming Philanthropist Nels?"

"The very one," I said. "But he didn't kill all those people himself. It was more like he...insinuated the idea into people's heads, then offered them ways to make their deepest murderous inclinations come true. Although he never explained what happened to Corey. Maybe he did kill him in the end, just to tie up loose ends, as it were."

Nels appeared in the doorway in handcuffs, and Titan pushed him forward down the steps. I wished I could magically disappear, but Nels' eyes met and held mine. He didn't say anything as he walked my way, but once he got closer, he mouthed the word, "Leo."

I scooted backward as if I'd been hit, and Titan shot me a concerned look. He hadn't witnessed Nels' parting blow. I gave him an encouraging nod, anxious to see the man get whisked away by a police car.

Once Nels was situated behind the bars of the police cruiser, an officer walked Chelsea out the front door. She offered me a sad smile as she headed for the ambulance. "Thank you for coming for me."

Kylie was carried out behind her, and she was immediately placed on a stretcher. Summer and I hurried over to her side. Her eyes were closed, but I was relieved to see her chest moving as she took shallow breaths.

I spoke to the paramedic. "It's her left elbow you'll want to check for a break." Lowering my voice, I asked, "Is she going to be okay?" Her prolonged state of inactivity seemed abnormal to me.

"She will be, ma'am. We think he gave her a hefty dose, but she's breathing just fine. We're going to fix her up for you."

The detective walked to my side. "I'll call you the moment they give her the all-clear from the hospital," he said. Turning to Summer, he said, "I do need to ask Macy some questions tonight. Were you planning to stick around?"

"Of course," Summer said. "I have her car anyway, so I'll take her home after."

All I wanted was a hot bath and some extended snuggle time with Coal. I could hardly bear to stand in front of Nels' ominous house for another moment. But I knew my duty, so I forced a smile. "Fire away," I said.

Titan was on his way over, and he seemed to notice my lackluster response. He turned to Detective Hatcher. "How about this, Charlie—what if I drove Macy home and asked her your standard questions? I could record her answers, then leave them with your assistant to transcribe when I come in for the interrogations tomorrow."

Summer raised her eyebrows, clearly intrigued by this turn of events.

The detective took another look at me. "What do you think of that option, Macy?"

I breathed a sigh of relief. "I'd love it." I couldn't wait to leave Rhododendron Drive and never come back.

THE LEATHER SEATS in Titan's big SUV felt so comfortable, I could barely stay focused. I had to apologize a couple of times for nearly drifting off in the darkness.

"No need to apologize. You've had a traumatic experience," he said, flipping the record button on his phone. "I just need to ask you a few questions. So, given what you've told me, it sounds like Nels Hartmann had a hand in Alec, Doug, and Emmy's deaths, but he didn't kill any of them directly. Is that right?"

"That's what he told me," I said. "He never explained what happened to Corey, but I figured he gave him some kind of drug that would kill him, then stabbed him to make things point toward Kylie again."

"But he got impatient waiting for Kylie to get convicted for good," Titan said. "You told me he hired a lawyer for Kylie when she was in jail—what was that all about?"

"I believe it was all for show, to throw suspicion off himself. After all, Bo was the one who posted bail for Kylie—not Nels. Nels didn't really *want* Kylie to get out of prison. Honestly, I don't know what kind of lawyer he had, but he might be crooked."

We pulled up to my darkened house. In our hurry to find Chelsea, I'd forgotten to leave a porch light on. My SUV sat parked along the curb, since Summer left before we did and took her own car home.

Titan unbuckled. "I think that's enough questions for now. Please let me walk you in."

I wasn't about to argue with him, since I was practically too tired to take a step. We made our way to my back porch, and when I unlocked the door, Coal ran out, not even pausing to sniff Titan.

"Guess he had to go," I joked, amused that my dog unquestioningly accepted Titan just like he did Bo. I flipped on the porch light.

"Thank you again for bringing me home," I said. "I know it was a short trip, but I don't think I'd trust my driving tonight."

"Understandable," he said. His light brown eyes peeked out from beneath his brown curls, which were on the longer side. The curls made him more approachable than when he had his hair cut short, although he still couldn't shake that authoritative, trained agent vibe. "We've been looking into Nels Hartmann for years. This is the break we needed, although I hate that you had to get caught in the middle of things. Given what you've told us, Nels might decide to squeal on Leo Moreau, and if so, that'll be the kind of solid evidence we need against him."

"Plus, Bo's got something," I said. "He told me."

Titan nodded. "If everything comes together, we'll be able to get Leo coming and going. That would be a huge win for our state."

"But you live in Virginia now," I joked.

"I'm still a mountaineer at heart," he said. His eyes were soft. "There are so many things I love about this place."

I took a deep breath. Surely he didn't mean—

"Macy, I was wondering—I'm going to be in town a few days for the interrogations. Would you like to get together sometime?"

I wanted to playfully ask, "Like a date?" but my tongue was frozen. I simply nodded.

"Great. What night works for you?"

Come to think of it, on Friday night I was supposed to be going on a walk with Dylan. Things were getting a little crazy around here.

Coal broke my weird silence by coming up the porch steps and sitting down at Titan's side. I had to smile as his tail pounded on the wooden floor. Since Titan was so tall, he was the only person who made Coal look like a normal-sized dog in comparison. Next to me, Coal practically looked like another adult.

"How about tomorrow night?" I asked, hoping I didn't sound too eager.

"Sounds great," he said. "I'll get going. Just text me what you want to do tomorrow. He smiled and was down the porch steps in no time.

I took Coal inside and locked the door behind me. I felt a

little dizzy with excitement. Titan had actually asked me out.

It was only as I was tucking into bed that I remembered I was meeting Jake at the cafe tomorrow at noon. I hated having to focus on my ex-husband before my date, but it had to be done. Hopefully he'd be on the fast track to South Carolina right after we talked. At this point, I honestly didn't care if he was seeing anyone else—in fact, I kind of hoped he would, so he would drop these misguided attempts to get back together with me.

24

DETECTIVE TUCKER TEXTED in the morning that Kylie and Chelsea had been released from the hospital. They were both feeling much better, although Kylie would have to have her elbow in a sling for awhile. Thankfully, the break had been minimal and would shift back into place without a cast.

I was surprised to hear that their mom was the one who'd picked them up. Maybe their relationship would start to heal, now that Kylie had learned the real reason her dad lost his job.

I thought about taking the day off, but since Bristol would need to start filling in for Kylie, I decided to go in. Summer had lots of questions for me when she came by, but I had nothing new to share, besides the fact that Titan and I were going on a date. This information brought happy tears to her eyes and she gave me a monster hug, although I cautioned her against getting too carried away.

As promised, Jake showed up at noon on the dot and ordered his lunch. After grabbing a turkey on rye sandwich and an iced latte, I joined him at the table near the fireplace.

His smile stretched extra wide as he said, "So good to see you, Macy. You're looking great."

I knew that was a lie. I'd overslept and hadn't had time to style my hair after blow-drying it, so I knew it looked like a puffy red cloud floating atop my head. "Thanks," I said, sinking my teeth into my sandwich. I didn't feel like rehashing any of the events of last night. Silence stretched as I waited for him to expound upon the reason for our meeting.

He took a couple sips of his tomato bisque soup, then pulled a folded paper from his jacket pocket and set it on the table. "I needed to ask you something," he said. "I was going through some things, and I found this old document in a box. It turns out that my dad gave us ten shares of stock in the dealership when we got married—in both our names. I know that doesn't mean much to you now, but I'd like to increase my stock in the company since I'll be taking over soon. Would you mind signing those over to me? I'd be happy to donate some of what they're worth to Barks & Beans."

I didn't see any reason not to. I had no desire to hold onto shares of Jake's dealership. But I certainly didn't want to be beholden to him in any way. "I don't want you donating anything to the cafe. We're doing just fine. But if you pass it on over, I'll be glad to sign."

He slid it my way, along with a pen. I skimmed the document, which seemed on the up and up, then scrawled my name on the line. I hoped this was the last thing he wanted from me.

"Thanks so much." He took another bite of his grilled cheese sandwich, and we ate in silence. I had nothing left to say to him. Jake was an exhausting kind of person for me to be around, since I never knew which tactic he'd use next.

This visit, he'd played the "I'm so sorry, I was wrong" card several times, and it struck me as utterly disingenuous. Anyway, we both knew it wouldn't be long before he found another woman who would hang on his every word. It was just who Jake was.

I wrapped up half my sandwich and finished off my latte. "Well, I hope you have a safe trip," I said, standing. "I'd better get back to work."

He jumped to his feet. "Macy, I—"

I cut him off. "Jake, you need to get home." I couldn't believe I'd once been held captive by those lying green eyes. I turned and headed for the Barks section, eager to get back to the dogs, who couldn't act deceitful if they tried.

WHEN TITAN CAME to pick me up at six, he had good news. "During questioning, Nels turned on Leo, and so did Leo's muscle guy. By the time Bo extradites his witness, we'll have plenty to take him down. Now we just need to locate Leo."

"He always seems to have hiding places," I said.

"Like any self-respecting crime lord," Titan said, chuckling. "But something tells me we've got our own personal homing device...his wife, Anne Louise." He pulled into the Italian restaurant we'd decided on.

"You know you can't trust her, no matter how helpful she is toward Bo," I said. "She's just using him to get her husband out of the picture."

"We know, and we're fully aware that we might be raising up a many-headed hydra that will be far more difficult to stop. Trust me, we're trying to stay ahead of her and lay the groundwork so she doesn't have a successful takeover." He smiled. "I couldn't resist that hydra reference—remember I told you my mom was obsessed with myths?"

"Thus your unusual name," I said, grinning.

Sunlight hit the golden flecks in his eyes as his voice deepened. "Macy, I don't think I've told you how lovely you look tonight."

My cheeks warmed at his compliment. Titan wasn't the kind of guy to throw compliments around, like Jake. When he said something, I knew he meant it.

"Thank you," I said.

He leaned back in his seat and stared out the windshield, as if choosing his words carefully. "I know I'm not the most...verbal person. It's a failing, really. I've told you I'm divorced, but the full story is that my wife left me. And she had good reason to."

I froze. He couldn't be a cheater, too.

"I never talked to her about things," he continued. "I worked all hours and traveled all the time. I didn't pay attention to her. How could a marriage be expected to survive that?"

Relief washed over me. Of course he hadn't had an affair. Although the marital issues he'd mentioned were serious, they were the kinds of things that could be improved on.

He seemed unwilling to look at me, as if shouldering a huge burden of guilt. I placed a hand on his shoulder, and he finally turned my way. His eyes mirrored the deep kind of sadness I'd harbored since the breakup of my marriage.

"We need to stop beating ourselves up," I said quietly. "Yes, we've both done some things wrong in our marriages. I blindly took what Jake said at face value, never asking the questions I knew I should've been asking. I let myself get swallowed up in his dreams, and I didn't fight for my own. I made excuses for him and let him buy my love with cheap compliments and expensive gifts. So we've both admitted what we did wrong in our marriages. That doesn't mean we're doomed to repeat the same mistakes, does it?"

He took my hand into his own. "You always seem to look at the bright side, even after all the hurt you've experienced." He leaned in so close I could feel the heat radiating from his polo shirt. "I don't know how you do it, but you have this...dauntlessness about you. You make me believe things can get better."

I gave his big hand a squeeze. "And thanks to you and Bo, I can still believe there are good guys left in the world who are fighting for what's right."

His gaze shifted to my lips, and everything seemed to slow down. There wasn't one thing fake about Titan McCoy, from his thoughtful words to the unconcealed admiration in his eyes. When he took my face in his palms, gently leaning down to cover my lips with his own, the force of a thousand unspoken hopes washed over me.

Because a kiss from Titan felt like a promise, and the kind of loyalty he offered was something I'd never take lightly.

OVER LASAGNA, Titan opened up more about his failed marriage, and I wound up venting much of the pent-up anger I'd been feeling for Jake. It felt like a glorious catharsis, and a positive step in the right direction. As I polished off my meal, I knew I was going to have to talk with Dylan about Friday night. I couldn't go out with him when I felt such a strong connection with Titan.

After our dessert was served, I told Titan that Jake had been lingering around town. "I think I finally got rid of him, though," I said. "He wanted me to sign over some stock shares his dad had given us in their company when we got married. I was only too happy to do it."

"Is it a large company?" Titan asked, sipping at his decaf.

"Just a used car business," I said. "Jake's taking it over, so he wanted the shares so he could increase his ownership interest."

Titan looked thoughtful. "Did you ask him how much those shares are worth now?"

I shook my head. "I frankly didn't even care. I just wanted him to leave."

He raised an eyebrow. "That...feels a little like manipulation," he said. "You might want to check into Jake's car business a little more."

I shrugged. "That's the agent in you talking. Not everyone's on the take."

Titan looked serious. "Yes, but from what Bo has told me, Jake generally is."

He had a point. Had I been hoodwinked by my ex again?

TITAN WALKED me to my door, where he leaned down and gave me another tender kiss. I headed inside, feeling like my entire world was wrapped in a happy golden haze. I gave Coal an enthusiastic head rub before sweeping Stormy into my arms for a little kitty TLC.

It seemed unbelievable that the man I'd been fascinated with since the day we'd met had said he was every bit as fascinated with me. We were actually heading toward a relationship.

But after taking a long bath and pondering what Titan had said about Jake, I knew I needed to check into what was going on with his car business.

I couldn't ask either of his parents for details. After all, they had always backed their son, even when he'd blatantly admitted to cheating on me.

There was one person who might have a beef with Jake, though, and that was his ex-secretary, Sherry Dunford. I felt certain she'd been fired from the dealership because Jake had decided to drop her, just like he'd dropped me.

Shockingly, I'd kept her number plugged into my phone. It was ironic that I used to call her at the office to find out where Jake was, and most likely, he'd been with her every time.

I shoved my black thoughts down and sent her what I hoped came across as a friendly text. "Jake came to town and seemed interested in making amends. I wanted to check and see if he was telling the truth that he wasn't with you."

She fired back with a quick response. "He dumped me for another girl. Don't believe him."

So he had misled me, making it seem like he was once again a free agent. "Who's the girl? Is she at the dealership?" I asked.

Sherry's text response was scathing. "He's moving up in the world now that his business has gone statewide. He's set his sights on Carlee Riggs. Her daddy's Gary Riggs, who owns a lot of businesses around."

I texted back, "What do you mean, statewide?"

It took little longer for her next text to ping. "Didn't he tell you? His dealership was recently bought by a big company. It's going to be a statewide chain that might even go national at some point. Jake is playing with the big boys now."

I thought she'd finished, but a final text sounded from her. "From one woman to another, you should stay as far away from that two-timing snake as you can get. I have to run. Bye."

I found it bleakly hilarious that the woman my husband had cheated with was now warning *me* that he couldn't be trusted—even using my own nickname for him. And yet he was so very like a snake...

Titan had been right. Jake had come to town with an ulterior motive—to get me to sign those ten shares over to him. Their value was about to skyrocket, and he wanted to keep every penny for himself.

Once again, he'd betrayed me without even batting one of those beautiful green eyes. Even though I'd thought I was in control of the situation, keeping my distance and finally ordering him to leave, he'd been playing me like a cast-off violin the entire time.

As I dropped onto my bed, Coal came over to nudge me with his nose. Grabbing my journal from a drawer, I began to write down all the ways Jake had gone about smooth-talking me into doing exactly what he wanted. I needed to remember this experience in case he ever decided to walk into my life again. Next time I wouldn't listen to one word he said, because his spell over me was most definitely broken.

25

A WEEK LATER, Summer and I met Bo at the airport, subjecting him to countless hugs. His hair had grown out, and his red beard was full and bushy. He wanted to drop by the cafe on his way home and see how things were going, especially with Kylie. She'd only recently returned to work, and, although she still favored her healing elbow, she had a new kind of enthusiasm about her.

From what I could tell, Joel had been driving up each weekend to check in on Kylie. Once, I even overheard him reading classical poetry to her on her lunch break, and instead of pulling into her shell like she used to, she was leaning forward, drinking it in. Her near-death experience seemed to have given her a new lease on life, and I was happy to see it.

Bo was welcomed into the cafe with open arms and a huge strawberry shortcake that Charity had made just for his return. The employees gathered around him like he was some kind of superstar, and even Vera dropped by to give him a big hug. "I have a pot of cabbage rolls made for your supper, along with some cornbread," she said. "Be sure to pick it up later. I can't wait for you to see Waffles."

When Vera started chatting with Charity, Bo raised an eyebrow at me. "Does she mean *that* Waffles?"

I nodded. "It actually seems to be a match made in heaven."

After catching up with everyone, Bo and I walked over to my place to pick up Stormy's things. The moment I opened the door, the cat must've realized her owner was in the house, because she came tearing downstairs at top speed. Coal made his way to my side, silently observing the joyous reunion of kitty and man.

With Stormy cradled in his arms, Bo turned to me and said, "Now, do you want to tell me about you and Titan, or do I have to piece things together from the liberal hints Summer's been dropping?"

We sat down on the couch and I shared about the relationship developing between Titan and me. I was surprised when Bo fell silent.

After a moment, he said, "You know Dylan's a friend of mine, too, and I feel like he thought you two were—"

I nodded. "I know. I wasn't sure *what* we were. But we met up at the cafe to talk about it, and he was really understanding." I thought back to our conversation earlier in the week. Although Dylan had called me the "entire package" and said he would never fall so hard for anyone else, he did agree to my suggestion that we continue our friendship.

Bo finally gave an approving nod, which spoke volumes. "Well, Titan's a great guy—not like Jake in the least. Your taste has vastly improved."

I took a deep breath. "Speaking of Jake, I didn't quite tell you everything that happened when you were gone."

As I shared about Jake's visit, Bo's leg started bouncing like he needed to go for a run. By the time I got to the part about Jake taking my stock shares, he jumped to his feet. "What a lying little coward," he spat out. "I'd better not ever see him in this town again, Macy, or I swear—"

"I know, I know," I said, trying to defuse his anger. "Now it's your turn to tell me all about the guy you found in Ecuador."

My distraction technique worked, because Bo launched into his story of Carson, the crooked official Leo had been paying off. After Bo had done some 'cajoling'—which I suspected might be a euphemistic term for more forceful DEA techniques—Carson had agreed to turn against Leo. The man had years of documentation on the illegal drugs he'd run into the States for Leo.

"It's a matter of time now," Bo said. "Carson, Nels, and that muscle guy called Little Ned, are all going to testify against Leo. For years, he's broken every law you can think of, but nothing ever sticks to him. This time, he can't weasel out of it."

I leaned into the couch, stroking Coal's glossy head. "I know it must feel good to have played such a big a role in finally taking him down."

"It does. And things are happening fast, because when Anne Louise found out I was back home, she called and told me how to locate the island where Leo's holed up. The FBI is already on their way to retrieve him."

I frowned. "Doesn't it raise your hackles to realize that she knows where you are all the time? She's just as bad, if not worse, than Leo."

Bo shrugged. "She's working on our side. You know what Auntie A used to say—'Don't look a gift horse in the mouth.'"

I had a feeling Anne Louise Moreau's "gift" was going to turn into something more like the Trojan horse. But for now, I was perfectly content to hang out with my brother and our pets, catching up while we ate cabbage rolls and cornbread.

It was time to let the shadows of my marriage fade and start enjoying the dream I was already living.

Preorder Heather Day Gilbert's next Barks & Beans Cafe
cozy mystery
TROUBLE BREWING

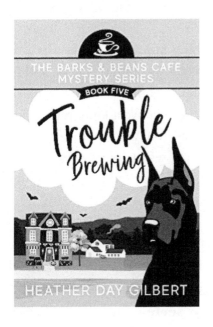

**Welcome to the Barks & Beans Cafe, a quaint
place where folks pet shelter dogs while enjoying
a cup of java...and where murder sometimes
pays a visit.**

Convinced that the elderly lady in her care didn't die of
natural causes, Macy's friend Della determines to look into
the broken relationships surrounding the woman. She books
a Halloween-themed getaway at a local inn and talks Macy
into coming along with her to spy on her prime suspect.

As they join a ghost tour of the candlelit town, Macy and Della feel their guide is a little too fanatical as he shares his spooky tales. He tells the story of the Greenbrier ghost, a newlywed who supposedly came back from the grave to tell her family that her husband murdered her.

When a disturbing apparition makes its presence known, guests at the inn become apprehensive...and for good reason, because soon after, a young bride turns up dead. Although everything points to a copycat killer replicating the historical Greenbrier murder, Macy has her doubts. She's discovered that the inn harbors secrets of its own, and when she pokes into one darkened corner too many, she might not stand a ghost of a chance.

Join siblings Macy and Bo Hatfield as they sniff out crimes in their hometown...with plenty of dogs along for the ride! The Barks & Beans Cafe cozy mystery series features a small town, an amateur sleuth, and no swearing or graphic scenes.   Find   all   the   books at heatherdaygilbert.com!

The Barks & Beans Cafe series in order:
     Book 1: No Filter
     Book 2: Iced Over
     Book 3: Fair Trade
     Book 4: Spilled Milk
     Book 5: Trouble Brewing

Be sure to sign up now for Heather's newsletter at

heatherdaygilbert.com for updates, special deals, & giveaways!

And if you enjoyed this book, please be sure to leave a review at online book retailers and tell your friends!

Thank you!

Made in the USA
Las Vegas, NV
15 June 2021

24826432R00132